CARRICK ROADS

A DCI CLAIRE CORNISH MYSTERY

F G LAYCY

It doesn't make for sanity, does it, living with the devil.

Rebecca, Daphne du Maurier

Dead men tell no tales, Mary.

Jamaica Inn, Daphne du Maurier

Table of Contents

Preface	6
Chapter One	8
Chapter Two	14
Chapter Three	20
Chapter Four	28
Chapter Five	37
Chapter Six	40
Chapter Seven	44
Chapter Eight	49
Chapter Nine	53
Chapter Ten	59
Chapter Eleven	62
Chapter Twelve	71
Chapter Thirteen	74
Chapter Fourteen	79
Chapter Fifteen	83
Chapter Sixteen	90
Chapter Seventeen	98
Chapter Eighteen	110
Chapter Nineteen	115
Chapter Twenty	118
Chapter Twenty-One	124
Chapter Twenty-Two	128
Chapter Twenty-Three	132

Chapter Twenty-Four	141
Chapter Twenty-Five	150
Chapter Twenty-Six	162
Chapter Twenty-Seven	167
Chapter Twenty-Eight	174
Chapter Twenty-Nine	180
Chapter Thirty	184
Chapter Thirty-One	194
Chapter Thirty-Two	202
Chapter Thirty-Three	206
Chapter Thirty-Four	215
Chapter Thirty-Five	218
Chapter Thirty-Six	222
Chapter Thirty-Seven	229
Chapter Thirty-Eight	233
Chapter Thirty-Nine	236
Chapter Forty	238
Chapter Forty-One	244
Chapter Forty-Two	248
Chapter Forty-Three	251
Chapter Forty-Four	257
Chapter Forty-Five	263
Chapter Forty-Six	271
Chapter Forty-Seven	276
Chapter Forty-Eight	282
Chapter Forty-Nine	287

Chapter Fifty	303
Chapter Fifty-One	307
Chapter Fifty-Two	311
Copyright © FG Laycy 2019	321
Author's Note	322
Bio	323
Acknowledgements	324
Other fiction books by F G Laycy	325

Preface

It was the night of January 7, 2018, St Winebald's Day, and an ill wind whistled through the Cornish coastline as darkness descended upon the Duchy. Bodmin Moor was a remote, bleak heather covered granite moorland still grazed by moorland ponies and sheep.

The leader of this Pagan community wanted to reintroduce the old practices. The group of Satanists gathered by the great Hurlers stone circles close to the village of Minions. There was nobody else around to witness the sacrifice. The animal had already been subdued and now lay down on the mossy ground. This once regal Shetland gelding, already castrated, if that were any consolation to his owner, would be spared the usual removal of his testicles during his sacrifice. Instead, his eyes were gouged out, his teeth removed, and the rest of his genitalia hacked off before being disembowelled.

Their leader felt empowered. If he denied the power of magic, after having called upon it successfully, he would lose all he had obtained. He had harnessed that magic power, and along with the other Eleven Satanic Rules of the Earth, he had taken his revenge through this sacrifice. With the ritual completed the small group dispersed back into the shadows and silently left.

Chapter One

Every evening at 9 pm Roger Pascoe made two cups of milky Ovaltine. He lifted up the simmering plate and placed the old stainless-steel saucepan on the cream four oven Aga that took centre stage in the spacious farmhouse kitchen. Leaving it to come up slowly to a simmer Roger walked into the bathroom to help his wife Lowenna into the bath. Holding her under both arms, he pulled Lowenna roughly out of her wheelchair, swivelled her around and sat her on the reclining bath lift chair before swinging it over the bath and lowering her into the warm water. She enjoyed a soak to ease the stiffness and crippling pain in her body.

Roger had killed plenty of cattle and sheep in his time, but he'd never killed another human being with his bare hands. Roger couldn't stand his wife. He'd detested the lazy bitch for years. Her arthritis had deteriorated over time, and she now used a wheelchair - his punishment, or so Roger thought, for continuing his affair with his mistress,

Loveday. To this day he wished he'd walked out on Lowenna years ago rather than shut up and put up for the last fifty miserable years.

He added the milk to the mugs and slowly stirred in the Ovaltine powder contemplating his future and working up the courage to commit his heinous crime. Psyching himself up, he walked back into the bathroom. He would not bottle out a second time. Lowenna's eyes were closed as he walked up behind her. A shadow fell above her, his face, invisible to her closed eyes but she heard his voice.
'I'm sorry. You have to believe that.'
Lowenna opened her mouth, but no sound came out as Roger placed his hand on the top of her head immersing her slowly under the water. Unable to move her crippled hands and arms there was no resistance as Lowenna's nostril's and mouth were submerged. Her snatched breaths became rapidly shorter and shorter until she fell silent. Death did not come easily for Lowenna, but in those lingering five minutes before the light was extinguished, she smiled as she thought of her final retribution. Roger

walked back into the kitchen leaving Lowenna lying in her underwater coffin and sat down at the farmhouse table to finish his Ovaltine, in peace. He wasn't in a hurry; that was when mistakes were made. No, he wanted to prepare himself for the next part of his plan.

Lowenna's lifeless body was no longer in pain – at least that was some consolation. He emptied the bathwater and moved her corpse into the recovery position on the bathroom floor in an attempt to feign the clearing of her airways before ringing Doctor Mickey.

The family GP from Fowey River Practice arrived within ten minutes smelling of his usual brand of whiskey. He enjoyed a few drams each evening of the Balvenie Double Wood, a 12-year-old single malt scotch whisky.

Doctor Michael Mickey had known the Pascoe's for years. He'd even attended their wedding. They had all been young, full of ambition and hope for what the future held. Had they known what path their lives would take they probably wouldn't have cared or given much thought to their destiny at such a young age.

The Pascoe's had recently celebrated fifty years of marriage. The celebration had been a farce. Everyone knew Roger had been playing away from home for years. His mistress was even at the party under the guise of an old family friend to anyone who wasn't in the know.

Lowenna had turned a blind eye to Rogers bit on the side. Initially she had expected it to trickle out like all the others, but instead, it had lasted almost as long as their marriage and through births, deaths and illness. Lowenna's debilitating arthritis had been her curse and her sanctuary, limiting her life to be wheelchair bound and stuck in the confines of her home, sparing her the ridicule and gossip in the town. Everyone felt sorry for her rather than pity. She wanted neither, only revenge.

Loveday's husband had died from a sudden heart attack in his fifties, and at the same time, Lowenna had succumbed to being bedbound from her debilitating and painful illness. The only obstacle that had stood between Roger and Loveday finally being together had now been removed.

Mickey sat down at the table while Roger fetched out the bottle of whiskey and two glasses. Not a word was spoken until Mickey spoke up.

'She's at peace now and not before time. She was a tough old bird. Have you told the girls?'

Roger and Lowenna had two grown-up daughters. They were a disappointment in one way or another: Selfish, greedy, both wanting their piece of the pie and not wanting to do a day's work in return. They blamed Roger for any of their shortcomings and had sided with their mother over the years, their sibling rivalry set aside where their father was concerned.

If Roger had taken a good look in the mirror, he would have recognised himself in his offspring. He'd, after all, inherited his wealth from his parents who'd adopted him as a child from a poorer relation abroad and he hadn't done a proper day's work in his life since leaving school at fourteen, swanning around until both of them succumbed to early graves within weeks of each other. Roger had counted his blessings that natural causes had accounted for their demise on the death certificates issued by a young Dr Mickey. Since that day he'd enjoyed all the trappings of his inherited wealth and kept Mickey in a manner to which he'd now become accustomed. Having a GP in his back pocket would once again pay off. He didn't have to explain to Mickey.

They both sat in silence reminiscing and drinking until finally Mickey sat up straight and declared.
'Well, I suppose we had better get this show on the road. I'll call it in.'

Chapter Two

Claire Cornish rolled over in bed. Lying next to her on the super king bed was Englebert, his head resting on the other pillow. Being single had its advantages. There was no one around to apologise to for any gaseous escape, and Englebert was more than capable of holding his own.

Detective Chief Inspector Claire Cornish had taken advantage of an early night to catch up on sleep when the telephone started ringing. Heavy-lidded, the results of an earlier bottle of red wine, she talked to herself as she grabbed the receiver.
'Cornish.'

'Doctor Mikey here Cornish. I'm at Lankelly Farm. Lowenna Pascoe's dead. Drowned in the bath by the looks of it. I think you should get over here ASAP.'

Claire quickly dressed for the cold night and grabbed her car keys. Englebert opened one eye to watch her close the bedroom door behind her.

The beige Volkswagen RHD Poptop 4 berth Camper, an import from South Africa, was her prized possession sitting on the drive. Refurbished in Banbury, Oxfordshire, the 1903 cc engine with twin Dellorto carburettors and was her pride and joy. Few vehicles had gained the iconic status of the VW, and there were none which engendered quite such affection. A most unusual car for a DCI but practical as hell when a pit stop was called for and nifty around the Cornish lanes.

Ten minutes later Claire Cornish was standing in the Pascoe's bathroom looking at Lowenna Pascoe's arranged body. Rigor Mortis had not yet set in, and she took in the full scene before there were any further disturbances to the body and room. Roger had already admitted to moving her out of the bath and onto the floor.

Lowenna's naked body appeared to show no outward signs of any struggle, and there were no apparent injuries. There was no visible bruising, but then it was too early for that to be seen. Roger Pascoe was still sitting at the kitchen table with an empty gaze on his face which Cornish interpreted as being distraught at discovering his wife – dead.

Cornish pulled out her mobile phone and punched in the call to Detective Chief Superintendent, Jane Falconbridge, Commander for Crime and Justice in Devon and Cornwall Police. She had previously served as the Policing Commander for Cornwall and the Isles of Scilly. An experienced Firearms Commander, DCS Falconbridge had gained invaluable experience across different areas of police work including crime investigation, operational policing, safeguarding and intelligence management. She had a keen interest in promoting women in policing encouraging them to take on leading roles in the Devon and Cornwall Police. Maintaining a strong leadership and management was her primary focus, and she viewed Cornish as her protégé.

'Falconbridge.' The familiar Dorset tone came down the line.

'It's Cornish, ma'am.'

There was an imperceptible pause.

'Is this a social call?'

Cornish ignored the question since she happened to know that Jane Falconbridge liked to be the first to be notified and updated on any incidents, no matter how petty and at any time of the day or night.

'Ma'am, there has been an incident at Lankelly Farm. I was the first to be notified by the cadaver's GP. I've taken a preliminary statement from the husband and the doctor to confirm the death of one, Lowenna Pascoe, a sixty-eight-year-old female. It looks like an accidental drowning, but the medical examiner will need to establish the fact. I'll call in Detective Sargent Alex Hutchens.

Cornish had a soft spot for Hutchens who was old enough to be her own daughter and brought out her maternal instinct. Plenty of women police officers had worked under

Cornish during her career, but Alex Hutchens background brought back painful memories. They had a lot more in common than being just police officers.

Hutchens arrived with two more crime scene officers in tow, Detective Sargent, or DS, Gary Pearce and Detective Constable, DC, Dave Mac who were working the evening shift and had little else to do.

At her desk at Police Headquarters in Middlemoor, Exeter, Devon, Jane Falconbridge leaned back in her executive black leather reclining chair. DCS, Falconbridge, now had to maintain the modern police force with mission statements vision and values set out in the national Code of Ethics. It was a media nightmare in political correctness that she undertook daily to ensure her staff embraced current policies.

She considered Cornish to be one of her best DCI's. She was fully aware of her background and over the years had watched Cornish work tirelessly to achieve her position within the Police force. Being a cautious, meticulous overachiever herself Falconbridge was concerned that Cornish was too devoted to her career possibly to the extent that she had no time for any other social activities and to mull over the past. We all have our crosses to bear Falconbridge thought as she closed the file on Cornish.

Chapter Three

DCI Cornish was on her second cup of tea when DS Hutchens, DS Gary Pearce and DC Dave Mac walked in.

DS Hutchens was at the peak of her career, young and enthusiastic and looking for the next promotion whereas DS Pearce had no ambition or desire to rock the boat with his pension on the horizon. DC Mac was finding his feet in his new position.

Hutchens was a young, brilliant officer, in her early thirties and in many cases was more effective at dealing with disorder than the men. Her superiors, both strong women, encouraged her, determined to see that women remained a valuable asset to the force. Having joined at the age of 22, she quickly learned her trade working in the tough, deprived areas in uniform roles, such as on response teams and neighbourhood policing before progressing to all areas of crime investigation in the West Midlands police. The long, unsociable hours and on call meant she had little time for friends and boyfriends. Having passed her sergeants exam, and among the top one per cent in the country, she recently transferred to the Devon and Cornwall Police, more for personal reasons than her career – to find her birth mother. She had been adopted at birth and hadn't even realised she was adopted until her elderly parents were killed in a car crash eighteen months ago. Sorting through her parent's paperwork, she had found the adoption letters. Alex had always assumed that her parents had just had her late in life because of their demanding careers. It had never occurred to her that she wasn't their biological daughter. Now she wanted to find her birth mother and reconnect.

DS Pearce, on the other hand, considered the role of police officers had changed beyond recognition and that policing the last few years had lost its authority with the general public. Known to reminisce, especially after a few pints, he would often repeat to those that would listen.
'We used to be the heartbeat of a community with the bobby on the beat in my heyday. Communication virtually

stopped when the panda car took over, and there was no focal authority walking the streets. Instead, the paperwork has become the bane of a police officer's life as the force is no longer run by the Chief Constable but bureaucratic government officials.'

Pearce knew he didn't measure up to the requirements in the modern and ever-changing police force. He'd enjoyed the beat and the endless cups of coffee with those under his care in the community.

'When I walked into a pub where blokes were fighting each other I would have been on my own. Christ, I was the collective enemy. Right lads, if anybody wants a scrap – I'm here. Not all of you, let's say three. Bloody hell, not you, you're too big for me. Before you knew it, you'd got them laughing. You'd start with them all wanting to rip your face off, and then end up having a pint with them all in your uniform. Now I'm stuck in a car, remote and no longer a trusted point of contact with the locals and thoroughly unhappy. I've given the best years of my life to the force.'

Pearce and there were plenty more like him who were typically old school, couldn't adjust to the changes, the influx of multi-racial, gay, lesbian and bi-sexual officers. He had been raised in a household which was staunchly anti-gay. To see LGBT officers attending and parading in Plymouth Pride grated him, but other than those who knew him well he kept his own counsel and personal view in check. The whole political correctness thing irritated him more and more.

DC Mac was a recent addition to the county and was one of the few LGBT police officers in the force and part of the Devon and Cornwall Gay Police Association promoting the police diversity recruitment programme. A former counter-terrorism officer, SO15, stationed at Heathrow airport, he had complained about homophobia in the ranks in Scotland Yard. Being gay he had suffered multiple counts of degrading and humiliating treatment in the Met. One officer had talked of gay men 'taking it up the arse', and another described him as being 'as gay as a gay in a gay tea shop' to which colleagues had greeted with laughter.

Mac had dreamed of being a police officer since the age of seven, and if it hadn't been for this latest appointment back in his home county, he would have stayed on sick leave. The tribunal which had ruled that he had suffered homophobic abuse in the Met had been a small victory in tackling prejudice among officers. In the backwaters of Cornwall Mac thought he would be able to put the past behind him. He hadn't banked on working with DS Pearce.

Cornish relayed her instructions.

'The ambulance is delayed, busy. An accident on the A30 has taken priority over our corpse. As the SIO, the senior investigating officer, I've already informed the duty coroner. The CO on call from the Coroner's office is Emma Bray. The Coroner's black van will do the pick-up. No point in the ambulance anyway. No one has touched the body since the assessment by the GP whose confirmed the victim is deceased. We need to preserve what's left of the scene and any potential evidence. The key witness is the husband, Roger Pascoe who was in the kitchen when his wife died. There appears to be no evidence of foul play but let's not rule anything out at this moment in time. Treat the scene as suspicious until we know otherwise. SOCO are on their way. Lucy Turner, the senior CSI, is on duty and no doubt a trainee minion. Ok, let's get on with it shall we?'

Cornish took down a brief statement from Roger Pascoe. There appeared to be no one else around, and no other party involved. Hutchens examined the bathroom while Pearce and Mac checked all the exits of the property for any possible intrusion. They didn't want to disturb any potential evidence. Turner hated other people treading on her toes, that was all except Emma Bray. Conjoined at the hip, the Turner and Bray duo, as they were known, were noted for their active participation in solving crimes in the area. Cornish considered them a formidable partnership.

CO Emma Bray turned up five minutes before the van arrived to remove the body of Lowenna Pascoe. She was an Assistant Coroner who served part-time while continuing to work as a solicitor. Bray enjoyed the diversity of the role, investigating each case and in some cases opening an inquest, the judicial inquiry into the death when required, where the cause was unknown or may not be due to natural causes. As an Assistant Coroner, she was a member of the judiciary and not employed by the Local Authority although they funded the Coroner's service and office staff. Her area now covered Devon and Cornwall. Cornish liked Bray for her professionalism and diligence. Easy going but thorough Bray was tenacious in court, and Cornish preferred her on the side of the law. She would have made a dam fine police officer.

Bray set down her bag and alongside Turner studied Lowenna Pascoe's body.
'Not much to go on here. Gilbert will examine the deceased more thoroughly back at base.'
The forensic pathologist in the area was Dr Gary Gilbert. He was about as fun to be around as the corpses he examined. Meticulous but painfully slow his overweight

frame belied his rapid turn of speed. Cornish had seen the man run and boy could he get a lick on when required.

Gilbert never offered his opinion before he'd spent time with his subject; he'd been caught out before and wasn't prepared to put his professional advice on the line.

'Bag her up. It looks like Gilbert's in for a busy night.' Cornish and her team left Roger Pascoe with Dr Mickey. Cornish felt sorry for the old man. Married for that length of time and to lose a loved one like that couldn't be easy. Roger Pascoe's two daughters had been informed. Strange that they had yet to turn up thought Cornish, but then grief affected relatives in different ways.

Chapter Four

Claire Cornish lived alone with her lemon and white Bassett Hound in Fowey, Cornwall in Honeysuckle cottage which overlooked Readymoney Cove. Considered ripe for redevelopment according to the local estate agents they'd approached Claire numerous times on behalf of keen Londoners wanting to snap up the prime property. Claire wasn't interested. She'd been born in this house and lived there all her life, first with her parents and then alone after they'd passed away. She'd been an only child. Fond of Bassett Hounds, Englebert had lived with Claire for the past eighteen months and had filled the childless void. He was four years old having initially lived with a young couple who'd found it difficult to cope with a largish dog when they had children. Englebert had brought happiness back into Claire's life, something she never thought would happen.

Honeysuckle cottage overlooked the sandy beach to the south of the harbour town of Fowey and the sea beyond.

Claire loved the sound of the waves as they gently lapped against the sand in this cove sheltered by cliffs. She could think of nowhere else she would rather live.

Cornwall in winter came into its own. Summarised as warm, often wet and sometimes wild Cornwall in winter was quiet, peaceful and still. The summer visitors had long gone, and instead of battling hundreds of families and tourists for a space on the beach Claire could appreciate the solitude on some of the best beaches in the county. Claire preferred this time of the year, sunshine could work its magic even in the ugliest of places like a pair of rose-tinted glasses, but Cornwall was God's country as far as Claire was concerned. When the sky was cloudy and grey, it complemented Cornwall's beauty adding a sense of drama and wilderness to the scene.

There was something romantic and idyllic about a winter walk on the cliffs and the stunning Cornish coastline. All wrapped up against the cold, a bracing walk was refreshing, and something Claire and Englebert enjoyed with the little free time Claire had.

The perfect picturesque village of Fowey at night was not quite the neon spectacle of Blackpool, but the twinkling lights were non the less illuminating and a welcome and homely addition to the port.

Being a local though had its disadvantages and advantages. The residents that caused the most problems hated her with a passion, and she was used to getting the occasional dog shit pushed through her door by unruly youths. Then there were the do-gooders who were always trying to fight a worthy cause and wanted her involvement. There was the church society, the local gardening club with their regular complaints on vandalism and the community council meetings which she attended each month in her parish and several others in the vicinity. Some of the local residents thought nothing of turning up at Honeysuckle cottage to moan or ask for advice.

Claire Cornish couldn't remember the last time she'd had a day off without someone knocking on her door. But she still wouldn't change a thing in her life. Claire's home was her quaint Cornish cottage stuffed with all her memories in this little piece of paradise.

No, Claire Cornish was content with her lot. At forty-six she considered that her childbearing days were over, and she would remain single. She wasn't quite ready to take on the mantle of the title spinster just yet. Her career was her life. She'd given up the chance of keeping her baby thirty years ago. A baby girl with red ringlets framing a cherubic face. Her parents had said it was for the best. No one ever mentioned the baby again, and Claire fought her own inner demons and guilt for giving up her daughter. There was never any question of counselling and the lad, her boyfriend, Jamie, of a year, moved with his family out of the county with his father's new job. That was the last she saw of the only person who loved her and felt as bereaved as she did. Neither had wanted to part with their baby, but they were in no position to support themselves, let alone a child.

Claire's relationship with her parents never fully recovered. They brushed the whole episode, as it was called, under the carpet. But, like any dutiful daughter and only child, she had continued to live at home except for the short spell at the Chantmarle Police Training Centre, Dorset which eventually closed its doors in1994.

Middlemoor was now the Police Headquarters and Police Training College. Ultra-modern and fit for 21 st century crime-fighting. The £29 million invested provided the operational headquarters for Devon and Cornwall and 40 police cells. The old cells were claustrophobic, these were spacious and utilitarian. All the cells had cameras, anti-graffiti surfaces, reflective ceiling domes so the occupants could be seen at all times plus low beds to prevent falls. There were no features which could be used for self-harm. The water supply could be cut to each cell to create a 'dry cell' for detainees who needed to be examined for forensic evidence. There were also accessible cells for disabled occupants and windowed cells for monitoring high-risk possibilities. With wider corridors to aid resistant occupants, cameras, intercoms and panic alarms the state-of-the-art new police facility was a showcase of modern design. The decontamination room with shower was used for cases where incapacitant spray had been used during the arrest, and there was a room with UV lamps for the detection of blood and dye from cash boxes. This was a slick one-stop shop.

Bodmin was the most recent modern building and headquarters of the police in Cornwall, albeit with no cells. There were six main custody units in Devon and Cornwall located at Plymouth, Exeter, Torquay, Barnstaple, Newquay and Camborne.

The ageing police station in Newquay, a sixties building with its perpetual odour of stale sweat and cleaning detergent, was the worst and in need of a facelift or completely rebuilding. The reception area had long gone which meant there was no way of gaining entry unless someone knew you were coming. Newquay was regarded by outsiders as one of Cornwall's main crime spots. Synonymous with tourists and the younger set attracted by the surfing beaches it displayed its fair share of lager louts, but the reality was far from the truth. Statistically, St Austell was Cornwall's crime capital, Truro came a close second followed by Newquay and then Penzance. Burglary and drug possession along with weapon offences were the most common with over 500 sexual assaults and only six murders in the last year. Cornish still considered Cornwall a safe place to live, work and visit and that the likelihood of becoming a victim of a crime was low.

Claire Cornish worked out of her Bodmin glassed office and liaised with DCS Falconbridge mostly over the phone. Exeter was only an hour up the A30 should she need to attend any meetings. Cornish owed her success partly to the support from Jane Falconbridge who had always put in a good word for her and steered her in the right direction. DSC Falconbridge was the only person who knew her past. The rest of her colleagues considered her tough but fair-minded, experienced and passionate about delivering a service to the community of Cornwall, and Devon and soon to be Dorset if the powers that be had their way.

Cornish knew the word on the hill, referring to Brown Willy, Cornwall's highest point on Bodmin Moor, was that DCS Falconbridge was going to head up the role as the Devon, Cornwall and Dorset police alliance operations commander if the scheme was approved by the Government. This would be a new merger between the two forces pioneering new policing methods such as the use of drone footage and a specially trained canine unit to sniff out computer hard drives and devices such as USB sticks and SD cards. The first digital trained search dogs outside the United States. Cornish knew it meant further Government cutbacks and merging the two forces would leave the police more stretched than ever. The police role was changing with new technology and in Cornish's opinion, not for the better. Senior officers' roles would be reduced, Operational departments would be aligned, and the administration and HR (Human Resources) and information technology departments shared, diluting the police's effectiveness in the long term. It was a change that Cornish hoped wouldn't take place.

Cornish relished her current position. She wasn't like DS Pearce, old school and neither was she like DS Hutchens, the new ethos. Cornish was somewhere in the middle where she still felt a connection to the general public yet had the modern facilities of DNA and advanced scientific facilities to catch those criminals that slipped through the net years ago. Cornish considered she had the advantage of a current force, combined with the balance of an ever-present public persona. Why change something that worked? Sometimes change wasn't for the better and like a lot of things in this world things had a way of coming around full circle.

Chapter Five

Dr Gary Gilbert had painstakingly finished his scrutiny of Lowenna Pascoe's body. He had scrolled through her medical history in detail, spoken to Dr Mickey, her GP, and read the police investigation report on file. The Home Office pathologist knew that no forensic pathologist would deny the fact that there was not one pathognomonic autopsy finding indicative of the diagnosis of drowning. The evaluation of a drowning, therefore, would be made by the assessment of the findings suggestive of drowning, the circumstantial details and the exclusion of other causes of death.

Gilbert always started without any preconceived idea that because the body had been found in water that drowning was the cause of death. He carefully examined clothing worn by Lowenna before she had her bath and then her body for marks suggestive of a struggle. Gilbert was looking for any loose or stray hairs, fibres and inconsistencies between post-mortem changes and the body's location. He had the photographs taken at the scene as evidence, and the decedent's hands and feet had been secured at the farmhouse before transporting her body to preserve evidence. DCI Cornish and her team with SOCO had done their job thoroughly at the farmhouse, and it was now his turn to build a picture of the events leading to and causing Lowenna Pascoe's demise. The only marks on her body were that of her husband and consistent with him aiding her in and out of the chair and bath. No other person had appeared to be present in the bathroom or on her body. Gilbert noticed that Lowenna had been roughly handled, but that wasn't enough to suggest she had been mistreated. After all, she was a rather large lady and would have required some effort to shift her body weight, in layman's terms, her lazy fat ass. He had some sympathy for her husband.

The internal examination included detailed microscopy in determining the nature, extent and stage of antecedent disease. A diagnosis of drowning required a full autopsy and toxicologic screening, histological analyses of all the organs including the lungs and the diatom test. Only then when all anatomical causes of death were excluded would Lowenna Pascoe presumed to have drowned. If the anatomic and toxicologic observations were equivocal, the opinion that death resulted from drowning would be merely presumptive and her death would be attributed to drowning only because the autopsy failed to disclose some other cause. He didn't like loose ends and ambiguity.

By the time Gilbert had finished his investigation, he was no nearer to establishing the true facts as the average person on the street. Without the knowledge of what actually happened in that bathroom coming to light, he had no choice but to declare that Lowenna Pasco had in fact drowned, and a verdict of death by misadventure was recorded.

Chapter Six

The funeral cortège drove slowly through the parish of Fowey. Roger Pascoe sat beside Loveday. He didn't care what his daughters thought. The family rift had been there for years, and he now had 'his other woman' to consider. The girls had refused to sit in the same limousine as their father and followed behind in the second two cars with their own families. Their mother had died, not a clean death or an in-between-the-sheets, holy water death but had drowned in the bath while their father sat in the kitchen. It wasn't as if he'd been left broken-hearted and near hysteria, overwhelmed with grief. The girls knew that their father had merely sustained the pretence of marriage preferring his secret liaisons of passion with his mistress. He had never requested a divorce, they had all been complicit in reality to what was going on. And somehow it worked. Lowenna couldn't bear his desertion so long as she was spared the shame of his infidelity. So, the truth was sacrificed to preserve her sanity and dignity. Better a fool's paradise of an illusion than a circle of hell.

That would all change with Lowenna's death and more precisely this funeral. The smallest of details of the cremation and the memorial service became a battle of wills with the girls. Roger relented. He placed his own obituary notice and disregarded their carefully worded version.

Roger insisted on his mistress claiming her rightful crown. Loveday had been content to be second place while Lowenna had been alive, but this funeral was to be her coronation and recognition of her role as Rogers partner. The family wanted her excluded. Roger was the enemy within, and his actions were seen as a betrayal of family solidarity. Loveday wasn't welcome regardless of their father's wishes. Roger was unconcerned.

As everyone gathered at the Glynn Valley Crematorium, Roger, flanked by Loveday, was determined to preside over the opposing court of his daughters and their families. For those at the Lowenna Pascoe's funeral, the grave represented an ending. For Roger, he saw it as a beginning of sorts.

Inside St Petroc's Chapel with its magnificent picture window and beautiful views across the Glynn valley, there was no crying; instead, there was a semblance of unity. In the stage-managing of Lowenna's departure and memories from this world, the family airbrushed Loveday from the picture painted in the reading. The girls' final blinding loyalty to their mother.

Lowenna's body had taken its last journey through the cremation chamber. The mourners filed out to the tranquil Gardens of Remembrance paying their last respects to the family.

With the funeral service over, tears shed, songs were sung, nobody wanted complicated food when their heads were already complicated enough with grieving and animosity. The nursey food and lots of cups of tea and coffee were handed out by the waiters and waitresses at the Fowey hotel. Roger had left the preparations to his daughters who amid their family and friends played their parts perfectly. Roger and Loveday exited the wake quietly, there was no point in antagonising the situation any further. There would be plenty of time for conversation and words that needed to be said at the reading of Lowenna's will.

Roger smiled. He and Lowenna had mirror wills leaving everything to each other. He would have the last laugh.

Chapter Seven

Maggie Boscowan and Nadine Pascoe were the first to arrive at Clemo Nicholl solicitors in Fowey with their children, Lowenna's grandchildren, who had been asked to attend. The girls naturally assumed that their mother had left each of the grandchildren something in her will, a memento, to remember her by.

Clemo Nicholl had been representing the family for years. Clemo was not only a family friend but had been one of Rogers ushers at their wedding. Roger arrived on his own. This was a personal family matter and didn't involve anyone else.

The animosity was palpable between Roger and his two daughters. He had a frosty relationship with his grandchildren, but that was understandable considering their mothers and the past. Roger thought Maggie had been too spoilt as a child and now expected that the world owed her a living. She used her family connections whenever she could and considered herself above most people. Maggie was the oldest and naturally assumed the role of the boss.

Nadine had been the apple of Lowenna's eye. An easy-going child, she simply did as she was told. Always happy to toe the line and acquiesce to keep the peace.

Clemo cleared his throat and read the will.
'To my husband Roger, who created my two beautiful daughters I leave you nothing from my half of the estate, you, money grabbing, lying cheating bastard. To my two daughters who insisted I change my will, I thank you. Following your advice, I leave you both equally the money in my bank account. The rest of my estate I leave to my three grandchildren, Barry Boscowan, Emma Hicks and Paul Hicks in equal shares.

There is a further clause, I might add here. The survivorship clause has been added to account for the circumstance of a beneficiary passing away during the estate administration as I assume this will be a bone of contention. This clause allows the testator to dictate where the assets should be redirected in this eventually. This clause states a set amount of time that the beneficiaries must survive them to inherit; this period is 28 days after the estate administration has been finalised.'

Roger listened in disbelief to Lowenna's detailed diatribe. The bitch had altered her will, and Roger no longer owned the farmhouse he was living in, only half of it with his grandchildren owing the other half. The rest of the properties would also be divided up. Lowenna had taken her revenge from the grave on all of them. She had not only altered her will but behind Roger's back legally changed the transfer titles of all the properties owned to tenants in common. Maggie and Nadine sat in stunned silence. Maggie was the first to speak.

'What the fuck just happened? I've been disinherited, and my only son gets a third of my mother's estate and Nadine's get two thirds? That's not fair.'

Clemo looked directly at his clients. The Pascoe's were the mainstay of his business in the area. They had shitloads of property previously from Roger's inheritance that had just been halved and divided among the younger generation of the family. Roger had lost half his heritage overnight. The children were instant multi-millionaires. Lowenna had the last laugh, her greedy daughters had been sidestepped.

Clemo knew his place and refrained from making any comment. He wasn't surprised by Lowenna's change of heart, and he had, after all, made the suggestions appropriately as her acting solicitor and advisor. The reality was that he didn't feel any of the family should have control and the benefit of the properties and wealth bestowed upon them. They were all in it for the money, they had no interest in the historical connections of their family and privileged background and did nothing to ensure that the wealth, hard-won and nurtured, would be retained and increased for the future generation, let alone cherished. Beautiful items of furniture, pictures and paintings had merely been trashed, ruined and left unappreciated.

Barry couldn't contain his anger. He by rights, as the oldest of the grandchildren, should have benefitted the most and been in control of the estate. Maggie grabbed Barry, and they stormed out of the room.

Lowenna had divided the family into a rift that was going to take the Clemo Nicholl Solicitor's business into another tax bracket.

Chapter Eight

Date: 31 January

The start of 2018 had been busy for Cornish and her team. Christmas decorations had just been taken down and put away for another year and events had already taken a turn for the worse in Cornwall. There was speculation amongst the locals that Devil-worshippers were responsible for the mutilation of the Shetland called Sonny on St Winebald's Day.

His owner said: 'He was opened up like a casket. The other horses were completely traumatised – they witnessed it. I found his body the next day. This was deliberate, and it was a sacrifice. Other animals have been mutilated in similar ways in the past, and there is talk about a cult in the area.'

Cornish made a statement to the public. She wanted to be quick to dispel the rumours that a cult was responsible. If it wasn't any of the locals, then the perpetrators had vehicles, but she didn't want the general public alarmed and on a witch hunt. The post-mortem on Sonny showed that he had been attacked with a blunt instrument which would have increased his suffering during the vicious attack.

'This area is remote. This may be the act of some random person or persons inflicting cruelty on this innocent animal. The police are investigating this serious attack. We are seeking any witnesses or information as to whom may be responsible.'

Cornish and her team had questioned all the locals in the village of Minions in a door to door enquiry. They all accounted for their whereabouts on the night in question. The 7 January had been a Sunday, and the pub didn't do meals in the evenings on a Sunday, only drinks and the usual crowd of three had been there propping up the bar. DS Pearce had made it his priority to attend and question those in the Hurlers pub.

According to the team's research the end of January and the beginning of February was an important time in the calendar of Satanists and tonight, 31st January, once-in-a-lifetime conjunction of a blue moon, blood moon and lunar eclipse. Cornish was concerned that if this were the work of Devil-worshippers, then they would be convening somewhere in Cornwall and Lucifer would be summoned, and a human or animal sacrifice would take place. The days surrounding the current super blue moon were also crucial in the Satanic calendar. If Cornish were correct then 29 January, St Agnes Eve would have been the prime time for the casting of spells, 2nd February, Candlemas (Sabbat Festival) would be another possibility for celebrating blood through animal and human sacrifice and the Satanic Revels on the same night observed satanic sexual rituals.

Cornish didn't believe in Satan or Demons, but she recognised that there were people who committed murder under the guise of evil as a reason for their actions. There had been plenty of inmates in the hospital in Bodmin, initially named the 'Lunatic Asylum' for the insane before becoming known as St Lawrence's. The iconic star-shaped building had now been replaced with new homes, and the residents left housed within the community in group homes, hostels and their own homes. Cornish was all too aware that unhinged people were walking among the normal population. They weren't all behind bars and known to the authorities.

Cornish had a hunch that the next couple of nights could be busy. She had a feeling that whoever was doing this had only just started and judging by the severity of the mutilated horse they had enjoyed themselves. She hoped she was wrong.

Chapter Nine

The Ship Inn was a favourite drinking hole among the locals and tourists in Fowey. The oldest pub in the Cornish port for more than four centuries and a safe haven for those cold nights around the large open fire which constantly roared during the damp winter months. It had recently been refurbished in shades of warm coral, red and grey, with the wooden floors reinstated to their former glory. Polished brass bar foot rails and elegant brass Captain barstools with leather padding framed the bar while comfortable plush captain seats enticed you towards the kitchen smells and homecooked food.

Roger was on his own at the bar. He'd driven down in his land rover, something he often did and would drive back the same route three sheets to the wind. It was common knowledge that the local farmers often frequented the public houses in their tractors and other farm machinery and by some fortuitous luck always seemed to make it back home safely, half cut.

Loveday was at her own home in Penzance. She suddenly had the desire, for the sake of decency, and with the death of Lowenna, to keep her distance, which was instead a surprising revelation and irked Roger. He didn't understand women at all. He had, after all, paraded her in front of his family and friends as a permanent fixture in his future. But, for some reason, which Loveday couldn't fathom, she wasn't quite sure if she wanted to be in Rogers life forever. She retreated to her family home and her children with the excuse that she wanted to put her affairs in much better order.

Roger suitably pissed off, and letting anyone know that would listen, drowned his sorrows with ale. Women were an enigma, he'd had two for the last fifty years and been faithful to Loveday for most of the time.

'What the fuck do women want? Now I'm a free man, where is she? You tell me? No, I tell you, Jack, you're better off being single mate. Don't get married. They fuck you stupid, then fuck with your mind when they marry you. I'm done with fucking women, you hear me?'

Jack was the fisherman come, barman, when the tide wasn't right. He'd never married, didn't see the point in it. He'd heard the same shit from all the blokes and decided it wasn't for him.

Roger continued to rant on, castigating most women as whores and only after his money. He had a nasty tongue when it suited him and wasn't liked, merely tolerated, which he didn't appear to register. Roger assumed most were jealous of his wealth and extensive estate of properties and land. He didn't realise that people found him to be obnoxious, overbearing and too full of his own self-importance.

Jack rang for last orders enquiring how Roger intended to get home.

'Don't be fucking stupid, the cars out front.'

Roger drove back to Lankelly farm rather the worse for wear. He parked his Landy as best he could after a few bevvies and tottered towards the front door. He managed to unlock the door and was about to walk into the kitchen when he heard footsteps behind him. He turned to see who was there.

'Oh, it's you. What the fuck do you want? Well, you'd better come in then.'

Roger, inebriated, slumped down at the farmhouse kitchen table and turned to his unexpected visitor. He watched, confused, as the caller, gloved, and speechless, bent down on one knee, unlocked and removed Roger's shotgun from the gun cabinet next to the porch and loaded it with three cartridges.

'Hey, that's my fucking gun. What are you going to do with that? Grown a pair of fucking balls, at last, have we?'

The late-night caller had done their research. Men were more likely to use firearms when committing suicide and aim for the head area while women tended to aim towards the abdomen. The uninvited visitor wanted this to look like suicide, not murder.

Roger, bewildered, didn't utter a word. As the night caller knelt down in front of him, Roger's hands were gripped, forcing him to hold the gun. Before Roger could resist, the barrel was encouraged into his mouth, and the single shot was fired from the pump action shotgun, upwards, blowing Roger's face clean away. Letting go of Roger's hands the gun fell onto the floor. Blood, bone, teeth and pulp splashed against the kitchen surfaces. The caller wiped off the splatter of blood and gunge from their clothing and calmly walked out of the farmhouse, closing and locking the door with their spare key. Failing to notice the shadow in the darkness they walked towards the direction of Fowey.

Having heard the gunshot, he watched the killer, illuminated by the occasional beam of light as the slow clouds passed across the moon, leave the farmhouse before looking through the window to see Roger Pascoe with half his head blown away. He couldn't make out the killer, but they had done his job for him. He turned and walked back to his car which was parked further down the lane, out of sight. There were no other homes in the immediate vicinity to hear the deadly shot.

He drove away listening to arias. The world order in Cornwall had been restored.

Chapter Ten

Satan or Demons were not bound to the 'full moon arrival' and were free to manifest as they desired. When he called a demon, it didn't matter what phase the moon was in. If he were sincere in his intention and approach, he would get results. They were calling the blessed guest from Hell, the first order of business when conducting a working. Tonight, was Candlemas, the Sabbat Festival and also a time for Satanic Revels which they celebrated with blood, animal and human sacrifice and Satanic sexual rituals. This was a double celebration tonight.

He called out.
'The Master of Darkness has ordered me. The king of demons is with us.'

The terrified young woman that lay in front of him was subdued. Her screams else would have awakened the village of Minions. Sound travelled with the wind on Bodmin Moor.

Naked and a virgin. He had chosen well. They disrobed and circled their victim like a pack of wolves. He would take her virtue, and they would all bathe in her blood. He parted her legs observing her mound of red hair matching her locks which fanned out from her head. Her eyes were green like those of a cat. He kissed her rosebud mouth and felt the saltiness of her tears. She was frightened, terrified, which increased his excitement. Raising her buttocks up with his hands he entered her moistness and rhythmically thrust his penis in and out watching her breasts rise and fall as he felt himself being drawn into her womb. The others watched and swayed as he embodied her body with his, eventually releasing his seed into the sac that encased him. Spent, he lay on top of his prize for a few minutes.

He was then handed the ritual knife, and as the others held her limbs down, he gouged out her eyes before proceeding to her organs, including her intestines and lastly her beating heart. Leaving the woman lying on the slab they bathed their bodies in her blood 'invoking the devil'.

He had been rewarded with success and financial gain, and this would now guarantee him even more.

Chapter Eleven

Roger Pascoe's body was discovered by his cleaner in the morning. Dr Mickey was at the farmhouse when Cornish arrived. Englebert sat patiently in the camper. He regularly went to work with his mistress and relished the fuss from her team.

Roger Pascoe's Land Rover was parked in the driveway of the farmhouse, at a peculiar angle. He had apparently driven in, just stopped and exited the vehicle.

Cornish walked into the farmhouse crime scene, along with her team assessing the situation. They were prepared for what to expect from her conversation with Mickey. Their job was to ascertain what had happened from the evidence presented and collected. She silently observed the crime scene, eyes sharp.

Turner accompanied by two other CSIs and Bray arrived at the bustling farmhouse. The perimeter had been sealed off.

This was the second time they had been to this location in a month. Shaking her head, Bray muttered.

'Death causes people to do unthinkable things.'

Turner appreciated the way Cornish dealt with her team. Efficiency and ensuring minimal contamination and disturbance of physical evidence. She was expeditious and methodical. Cornish had already made her job somewhat easier.

Everyone was clothed in personal protective equipment (PPE) to protect the scene, all except Mickey who was seated opposite his old friend, in tears. He couldn't believe that Roger had taken his own life.

'Roger was an experienced gun-user and always kept his guns in the cabinet.'

Cornish checked the gun cabinet. It was so secure the police couldn't get into it, and the key was missing.

Roger was slumped in the kitchen chair with the gun lying next to him on the floor and significant head injuries.

There appeared to be no suspicious circumstances surrounding the death from first appearances.

Roger's GP interrupted her train of thought.

'Roger may have had his faults, and he had a brief history of stress and depression a few years back, but there was nothing in his history to suggest that he had any plans to harm himself. Despite Lowenna dying.'

The SOCO team had been taking photographs of the scene and the body, placing yellow marker flags and collecting potential evidence. Cornish picked up the gun. It was in the locked position with the safety catch off and could not have been accidentally discharged. Black powder on the gun indicated that the weapon must have been very close or in contact with the victim's head.

The environment was secure, and Pearce has checked out the Land Rover and Roger Pascoe's movements during the evening.

'Roger spent the evening in the Ship Inn. Apparently, he was his usual rude self. On his own by all accounts and moaning about women. He left after last orders.'

Mac had checked the exits and the adjoining farmland and the lane.

'There are footprints by the farmhouse kitchen window, indicating someone had possibly observed Roger Pascoe, maybe the killer before he struck? We may know more from them. No other vehicles were in the driveway last night. It looks as if someone has recently parked down the lane, but then it could be a random car, unrelated, looking for a place for a bit of nookie. This area is popular with the youngsters, and the road leads down and eventually peters out to a walkable path onto National Trust land and the cliffs and the sea beyond. The only neighbour is half a mile away; they didn't hear a thing last night.'

Hutchens had the job of contacting Rogers next of kin. 'Roger has Loveday Pender as his next of kin. I've sent round someone from the area to speak to her, and she wants his girls informed. She'd like to be notified though where and when the funeral is to take place.'

Maggie Boscowan was Roger's oldest daughter. Maggie would be at home.

Cornish instructed Pearce to take Mac over to St Mawes. The look Cornish gave Pearce conveyed that he was to keep his mouth shut in respect of any comments regarding DC Mac's sexuality. Pearce wasn't well versed in being PC (political correctness) when it came to it. In fact, Cornish thought it would do DS Pearce some good to work with DC Mac.

Pearce enjoyed a banter, and if he was honest, he found it quite exciting to rattle Mac's cage. A tussle was fun, a little argy-bargy was harmless although he thought Mac far too over sensitive and wouldn't take kindly being the butt of any jokes. Being a snowflake and easily offended would make Mac's life difficult. Political correctness was not without its problems as Pearce, smirking, explained to Cornish.

'Bending over backwards to avoid offending others often backfires.'

The policy was just that, and they all had to tread carefully now with their work colleagues. Like the rest of the rules in modern society, they had to be seen to be doing the right thing. Cornish watched the two police officers leave together and hoped that they would each learn something from their generational differences to somehow bridge the gap.

There would be no easy way to tell Maggie and Nadine that their father was dead. There was no conclusion yet as to how Roger Pascoe had died. Suicide couldn't be ruled out, and until their findings had been investigated thoroughly by Gilbert and the police back at base, they were no closer to establishing whether this was accidental, intentional or deliberate – murder.

'Me and DS Hutchens will finish up here.'

Four eyes were better than two. All physical evidence had been removed or protected that could be compromised or perish by SOCO. Written preliminary documentation, notes, rough sketches and photographic evidence had to be permanently recorded before Cornish and Hutchens carried out the walk-through together to process the scene.

They had done all the preliminary collecting of evidence. Every piece of evidence had to be labelled and then whoever handled it now or in the future had to sign. The chain of continuity was vital. The CO van had arrived, and Roger Pascoe was bagged, tagged and sealed. Gilbert would be the next person to meet Roger Pascoe – on his slab.

The gun was carefully placed in the appropriately labelled firearm box and was a vital part of the evidence. The serial number was noted on the evidence tag along with the calibre, make, and model and the weapon photographed. The recovered ammunition was placed in a separate bag. Great care was taken to avoid damaging evidence or dislodging any related residue – blood, brains and any other matter.

The farmhouse was to be sealed and closed for the duration of the investigation. It was going to be one hell of a mess to clean up by the Crime Scene Cleaners.

Death tasted bitter, at any age. It was far more disturbing, grotesque. The last image of Roger Pascoe was of him dead, a gun on the floor and blood everywhere, chaos. Cornish felt that even Roger Pascoe deserved a better final snapshot than that. Cornish thought there would always be questions about his death that the family would probably never get answers to. She suspected that none of them really cared.

The family feud had only just started with Lowenna Pascoe's estate. Now there would be a second funeral and reading to add to the mix. Not that the Pascoe's were angels, far from it. Surely death and grief would hit this family. Cornish wasn't so sure. This bloody end could make people act kind of crazy and could seriously rock a family's centre of balance. With family misunderstanding and squabbles already evident, there would now be a further changing of roles and dynamics. Most relatives would grieve, albeit different styles, and have complicated emotions but Cornish felt this family would be divided due to Lowenna's will and their inheritance and now this. There would be no reconciliation with their father now he was dead.

Two deaths in the one family. Cornish didn't believe in coincidences.

Chapter Twelve

Gilbert was in his element. This case was right up his street. He'd completed his examination of Roger Pascoe under the microscope and could find no foreign hairs or fibres on him. His medical history gave a partial view of Roger Pascoe's state of mind in the past, and the only medication he was on was for his enlarged prostate.

He was running through his findings to Cornish. Gilbert liked an audience. The prints recovered at the scene in front of the farmhouse window were from a size 10 shoe. She noted his excitement in explaining the facts as he saw them. Cornish sensed that Gilbert was building up to a crescendo.

'The recent death of his wife would push any husband over the top.
What was interesting though was the barrel of the gun had been forced into Roger Pascoe's mouth. Having initially suspected suicide the post-mortem results didn't

substantiate that thought. The bruise on the victim's tongue was unique and consistent with blunt-force trauma. Something had struck the tongue, and the injury was definitely made before the shot that killed Roger Pascoe.'

Gilbert couldn't contain his excitement. Explaining to Cornish.
'If the barrel of the gun, a steel weapon, were placed in the mouth with some force, that would cause the bruising. The victim would not have done this to himself. Apart from the fact that the recoil from the shot shattered his top front teeth, blowing them out of his mouth. The shot went through his head, severed his spine and death would have been instantaneous and very messy.'
Gilbert liked to state the obvious with drama, something most peculiar to forensic pathologists; it went with the job.

'There was some bruising on the back of Roger Pascoe's hands indicating that while he wasn't restrained, he was gripped tightly, the shotgun placed and held in his hands to pull the trigger. The shooter was in control, the victim incapacitated from the high alcohol levels in his blood.'

Gilbert Paused looking for the spark of light in Cornish as she registered the thought.

'Roger Pascoe was murdered?'

Gilbert smiled with utter certainty.

'Absolutely. There is no shadow of a doubt. A cliché I know but the facts speak for themselves. Between 11.30 pm and midnight on the 2 February.

You have yourselves a murder.'

Cornish noted the date. Another death, possibly another sacrifice? This time human.

Chapter Thirteen

Funerals were meant to be a time for people to grieve and pay their last respects to a loved one. The family felt obligated to arrange Roger's funeral and attend. For years Maggie and Nadine had avoided parties and gatherings with their father unless their mother had insisted. They were all angry, but for the sake of appearances, they were forced to make peace for the day. Let's be honest, sometimes people die who you well, hate.

The procession left from the Fowey Hotel, it was, after all, mutual ground, each family in their own limousine, for the drive to Glynn Valley Crematorium. The family sat divided on either side of St Petroc's Chapel. They couldn't exactly slip in at the very last minute to avoid awkward small talk with the other mourners.

Cornish had now been to both funerals. She was beginning to feel something of an expert treading this strange dark path so many times. As the investigating officer, she often had to attend these events. If she was ever called to arrange a burial of someone, Cornish could do it with her eyes closed.

The family were aware of the police presence, and Cornish sat at the rear of the chapel. She wanted to watch the family as the minister conducted the ceremony. Was the killer sitting in plain sight? It was apparent to everyone in the chapel that the family were at odds. The animosity was palpable even to those that weren't well versed on the situation. There were hushed mutterings and tuts as Loveday turned up with her only son acknowledging Cornish as they sat at the back of the Chapel. At least she had the decency to take a back seat thought Cornish.

Maggie was relieved, and although she didn't display her other emotion visually, happy on the inside that her father had died. There was an immense sense of relief. And still, his death hadn't brought closure. The reality was that the pain of the difficult relationship she had with her father didn't die just because he had now gone. She would never get an apology from him. She had deserved that much. Nadine faced the front. She was all too aware of others staring at the family and the rumours circulating about who killed Roger. Maggie had stonewalled her since the reading of Lowenna's will and her physical removal from Nadine's life left an impact. Maggie was no angel, often too bullish towards Nadine, she still missed the contact even though the relationship was complicated at times. Maggie had got her through tough times; the human heart was funny that way. And yet, Nadine felt nothing, empty. She didn't want to speak ill of her father. Murder was a nasty way to die, and no one deserved that. Nadine knew once the numbness, and the anger had passed she may think of her father differently. Any unfinished business would now be left just that – unfinished.

Barry wasn't a hypocrite. He couldn't stand the man, his grandfather. He had no wish to mourn him. As far as he was concerned, he had been rude, a misogynist and a bigot which he had told him on numerous occasions. Even death wasn't good enough. He had deserved it.

Emma had only been to two funerals, her grandmother's and now her grandfather's. As far as she was concerned funerals sucked. Emma was here to say her final goodbye out of obligation, not respect. She was at the depressing event to get closure and put a bad situation behind her. Especially given the tragic way he died. Her grandfather had done some horrible things to her and Paul in the past, and they had never discussed it with anyone except themselves. It was their secret.

Paul was seated next to Emma. At the age of five, his grandfather had stolen his innocence, his trust in people and the world. All except Emma who had suffered the same fate. They had never told their parents. Their grandmother knew and had ignored it. Paul had pushed the events to the back of his mind. It was the only way he could cope with it. Sitting here brought back the painful memories. He was angry for not saying how he felt to his grandfather when he was alive. He was glad he was dead and had suffered a violent death. It was nothing he hadn't deserved. His punishment should have been greater. This was not justice.

Emma and Paul held hands throughout the service. When it had finished, they hugged each other to say everything would be alright. They had done nothing wrong. But you couldn't change the past.

Chapter Fourteen

Clemo Nicholl was having a busy month, Lowenna Pascoe's will was a bone of contention for the family. Maggie and Nadine hadn't spoken a word to each other since their last visit to this office. Maggie had already contested the will claiming that she had been unfairly cut out and wanted the will overturned regarding the unreasonable distribution of the assets to Barry, her only child. Clemo Nicholl had advised Maggie that Lowenna had made her will compos mentis, the will was drafted correctly, he should know, and Lowenna was entitled to disinherit whoever she wanted. Clemo Nicholl felt Maggie was greedy, after all, the grandchildren had inherited equally and therefore needed to work together if they wanted to receive their money which was tied up in the properties, estate, land and rentals.

They were now forced to be in the same room, once again, facing each other. The tension was like a razor blade – sharp.

Clemo Nicholl cleared his throat as if to bring everyone around to his attention.

'This is the reading of Roger Pascoe's will in accordance with his wishes. I leave my estate to my said wife, Lowenna Pascoe absolutely. Provided that if my said wife should predecease then my residuary estate shall be divided between my grandchildren, Barry Boscowan, Emma Hicks and Paul Hicks in equal shares, provided that; if any of my grandchildren die before me, then to divide that child's share equally between those living at my death. I leave nothing to my two gold-digging daughters except what is left in my bank account. They wished me dead instead of their mother. There is a further clause, I might add here, the same as in Lowenna's will; the survivorship clause has been added to account for the circumstance of a beneficiary passing away during the estate administration. This clause usually states a set amount of time that the beneficiaries must survive them to inherit; this period is 28 days after the estate administration has been agreed by all parties.'

In response to the will, Emma spoke up. The bitterness between Nadine and Maggie had rippled through the next generation. Roger hadn't seen much of Emma since a huge argument, and she had done her best to ensure she was never alone with him.

'I am unhappy that my grandfather won't be in my future, despite the past,' as she looked at Maggie who understood, 'but I'm even sadder that my grandfather should have been my hero and my protector, not some horrible, bitter dirty old man who I'm ashamed of. What's more upsetting is the falling out between our family over who gets what.'

Barry couldn't contain his anger and venom. His mother had insisted they stick to their guns. The law had, after all, left a window open for those that felt they hadn't been given their fair share of the inheritance. He intended to have it, one way or another. He stood up.

'We will never speak again except via Clemo. I'm not someone who's down on you both, referring to Emma and Paul, you got your equal share of the inheritance. I'm pissed because it wasn't divided fifty-fifty between both families. Why should I be penalised for being an only child when your slutty mother had two children. You're both laughing all the way to the bank. Well, I won't put up and shut up. I'll object to all your proposals to take money out of the estate unless further consideration is given to what I want.'

Lowenna had been dead for three weeks, Roger one. Maggie and Nadine had been cut off from both wills.

Clemo Nicholl suspected that the estate administration would not be reconciled for some time. With a family feud brewing, Clemo Nicholl was getting richer by the minute.

Chapter Fifteen

The gruesome discovery on Bodmin Moor near Minions, once again, sent alarm and panic throughout the small hamlet with its pub, restaurant, two cafés, and combined post office and shop.

Cornish with her boots squelching into what smelled like sheep dung or a cattle pat trudged up to the latest murder site. Pearce kept pace moaning about ruining his new shoes while Hutchens and Mac attempted to keep the press away and any onlookers in the busy carpark.

Cornish and her team now had two ritual killings to solve and the murder of Roger Pascoe. Two possible separate killers lose in Cornwall. The team would be stretched.

Turner and team and Bray turned up separately. Turner's crew erected a tent over the body and immediate area before the heavens opened and washed away any vital clues. A group of inquisitive sheep and cattle congregated on the edge of the area as if they knew it would be sacrilegious to venture any closer. There was an urgency to catching whoever was responsible for the recent deaths that reverberated throughout the whole force. Jane Falconbridge wanted results and fast and Cornish, and the rest of the team would be doing double shifts back to back and around the clock if necessary. There was to be no let-up and slack.

A young woman had been reported missing since last Friday night, and from the description given by the girl's parents, Cornish had now found their daughter. She hated this part of her job. Every time she got a call like this Cornish had to be objective and put on a mask to deal with the family, shattering their lives when the news was terrible. This was someone's child removed from this earth before their time.

It was at moments like this that Cornish thought of her only daughter and wondered where she might be. Was she even still alive or had some evil bastard hurt her? As her mother, Cornish should have been there to protect her own flesh and blood. Instead, she had discarded her to another, someone else to experience hopefully the joys of motherhood and the pleasure a daughter brings. Any mother's deepest fear was of losing a child.

Gilbert had performed the latest post-mortem, and the findings weren't pleasant reading. The victim had once again been subdued before being subjected to rape and mutilation.

'I found a couple of foreign hairs on the young woman's body, nothing else except fingertip bruising where she was held down but no prints. According to the pattern on her shoulders, arms, hands and legs I would say she was held down by several people wearing nitrile gloves. If I were a guessing man, I would say, two women and two men. The fingertip bruises on the upper body were lighter than the lower limbs indicating that the men restrained her legs and the women the upper body while the sexual act was performed by another male.

There appears to be only one different DNA sample from the hair. He used a condom when he raped her, and there was significant trauma to the genital area. There was no semen in her vagina, only the evidence of a lubricant that can be bought at any local chemist. The young lady's eyes were removed with a blunt knife and several of her organs removed while her heart was still beating at the time it was cut out according to my findings.'

Gilbert loved to embellish and gild the evidence with specifics.
'An interesting fact is that the heart follows a different pattern to other muscles in the body. The beating of the heart itself isn't regulated by the brain but actually within the heart itself. The only function of the brain is to tell the heart how fast it needs to beat. Nerve cells within the heart will continue to fire for an extended period before they shut down – prolonging the process of beating. For this reason, a heart that's removed from the body doesn't stop beating instantly. As long as it has enough ATP (Adenosine triphosphate) to provide energy and exposure

to oxygen, it will beat without any regulation from the brain. The human heart will continue to beat after it's been removed from the body for a short time.

In my opinion, both killings on Bodmin moor were carried out by the same person. The knife cuts are the same as the striations, and the mutilations were by someone who's left-handed. My conclusion is that both these murders were carried out by a man judging by the amount of force and if this were indeed a Satanic Ritual killing then he would no doubt be their leader. Find the girls killer, and you find the killer for Sonny.'

Gilbert had taken DNA samples. The police hadn't found a match in their system. The system used was IDENTI, the national automated fingerprint system that provided biometric services to the police forces and law enforcement agencies throughout England, Scotland and Wales. They could compare fingerprints and crime scene marks in a single database with a high degree of accuracy. Whoever he was he wasn't on their database.

The gory details were concealed from the press. Cornish didn't want a copycat killer. She had spoken briefly to the media about the latest killing of the young woman on Bodmin Moor.

Derwa Moon was from the Wadebridge area, and they had ascertained that her last movements had been at the Fishermans Arms in St Merryn with a group of young ladies on a hen night. She had been seen leaving with a young man. Her friends said that she wasn't 'that sort of girl' and assumed she must have known the person.

Cornish wanted answers and sooner than later. With a madman on the loose, it wasn't good for Cornwall. Minions was a favourite tourist spot, and the locals had expressed concern that the police weren't doing enough. 'Hutchens look into Derwa's place of work and let's see if we can connect her to any familiar faces and places. What does she do, hobbies, interests, previous boyfriends, relationships etcetera?'

Cornish addressed the rest of the team.

'Let's see if we can rattle a few cages. If this was another ritual killing which seems likely then when is the next one going to occur? The killer can't possibly think he can get away with this again in the exact same spot. So, he'll most likely look for somewhere else. What other places are there in Cornwall where ritual killings are most likely to take place?'

Pearce interrupted.
'I've been doing some research on the Satanic holidays. The next date in the Satanic calendar is the 15-17 March, the Eides of March, backstabber's day. A time to note the traitors around you. After that, it's Spring Equinox, Sabbat Festival, orgies and the like. Then Good Friday, Day of Passion (death of Christ) which is a blood sacrifice of a male adult and Easter Eve Day for human sacrifice.'

'Well, let's not sit around. Come on people, we're on a deadline.
The Devil waits for no one.'

Chapter Sixteen

Maggie Boscowan was hunched against the bitter wind as she walked her dog, Frank, from St Mawes harbour up to the castle and along Lower Castle Drive before following the footpath along the coast north to St Just. The sun was at her back with the wind pushing her swiftly in the forward direction. It was a crisp, fresh Spring day. She always felt at peace with the world when she walked this particular stretch of the coastline, with its splendid views over Carrick Roads, God's country. Maybe it was something to do with being close to St Just in Roseland church. Legend had it that Joseph of Arimathea brought Jesus to Cornwall and that he landed at St Just in Roseland. The church which was built beside the water on the tidal creek was arguably one of the most beautiful in the area and naturally the most photographed due to its assumed history.

Maggie liked to walk through the tropical vegetation, the fuchsias, hydrangeas, lilies and exotic shrubs. Paths meandered through the church gardens with its rhododendrons, camellias, azaleas, bamboos, wild garlic and bluebells, when in season. There were also several ponds with giant gunnera and small streams which rippled softly. The well-tendered grounds offered comfort to the relatives who visited their loved ones knowing that their graves were maintained and somehow enhanced by the tranquil and magical surroundings. Maggie enjoyed visiting her relatives that were laid to rest in their prepaid plots knowing that one day she too would be buried here. It was, in fact, the only thing she had ever planned for, her demise. It gave her some comfort. Today was the anniversary of her daughter's death, and as tears slipped down her cheeks, she laid a bunch of primroses on the granite stone engraved with her name, Demelza Pascoe.

There were so many secrets and so many times she had wanted to tell Nadine the truth. She had to live with what she'd done for the rest of her life. One of her mistakes was lying in this grave, the other was a walking timebomb.

No one else was around. Nadine, her younger sister, would never have forgotten the date before, but everything had now changed, and Maggie no longer cared about family. That wasn't strictly true, she just couldn't get past all the hurt and then the final disinheritance from her father. Steve, her husband, was enraged.

Maggie still enjoyed going to church and had done so ever since she attended Sunday school as a child although she struggled these days with the hidden demons in her closet. Assuring herself that she would make more of an effort with her husband she had every intention of addressing the issues currently at hand and getting her marriage back on track. The last weeks had been trying with family feuds and countless arguments on who should get what following their mother and now father's death. She'd hardly spoken to her father over the years and felt betrayed and angry following the reading of his will.

Heading back home in the same direction Maggie prepared herself against the wind. Keeping her head down, with her

Aran hat covering her unruly auburn hair, she dug her heels in, calling Frank to keep up as she strode with purpose. Slightly breathless she cursed herself for failing to adhere to her last diet in an attempt to shift some weight. Forty-something was meant to be the age where women felt thirty and rejuvenated. Maggie felt neither, worn down by recent events. She didn't smoke, the odd spliff now and then when the mood took her, and the opportunity, and a glass or three nightly of vino. Hence the reason why she couldn't lose her excess weight that hung around her waistline. Still, it didn't seem to stop her admirers who considered her sex on legs. Other women looked at Maggie and were enviable of her fabulous figure.

Her husband, Steve, was the Customer Commercial Director for Tulip Ltd, a meat processing company for all things pork and had recently earned a rare honour: Tulip's triple triumph. Now the proud recipient of McDonald's three-legged stool's supplier award for services to sausages.

The three-legged stool system was the backbone of the McDonald's supply chain, with each leg representing a vital component, i.e. the McDonald's company, the franchisees and the suppliers. Each leg apparently needed to be equally strong for the McDonald's unique business model to succeed. That was the cynical highlight of her year, Steve revelling in his award. Life couldn't get more exciting with Steve which was why she found herself in this situation. The only sausage Maggie now wanted was Jorey Pomeroy's. She'd tried to finish the relationship several times before, but each time she'd been lured back.

Steve was dependable, reliable, most of the time, and a good father and husband, yet Maggie was bored with her life. Yes, he had his problems and had managed to control his heavy bouts of booze. It wasn't often that Steve got out of his tree. He'd refused to go to Alcoholics Anonymous. They held a meeting in St Mawes once a week. He still wouldn't budge claiming he was a social drinker and didn't have a drinking problem. Maggie gave up trying to persuade him. After all, she was a social drinker and if the recent TV programme she had been watching was anything to go by then she was a borderline alcoholic along with a high percentage of the population. That was the least of her current problems.

Jorey Pomeroy offered her excitement and adventure. He enjoyed the wacky backy (cannabis) and had his own illegal still. He liked to live on the edge of society. She knew in her own mind that Jorey was only for now, not forever, she'd had her fun and soon she must end it before Steve found out, and everyone got hurt. It wasn't going to be that easy though with Jorey, and now there was a further complication with their recent Ménage à trois. Maggie had been enticed over to the dark side and had liked it.

Maggie didn't hear or see anyone approaching her with her head down until it was too late. Panting, both hands were placed on her shoulders to halt her steps. Maggie jumped, surprised, then pleased. She had been avoiding this confrontation all week, her infidelities had hit her like a ton of bricks. Her marriage was in crisis, possibly destroyed. And yet she had made no effort. She felt sick inside when she thought of all the affairs.

'You frightened me.'

Turning around she now faced him.

'You've been avoiding me?'

He was angry. Maggie had expected an apology.

'I can explain,' she shouted, desperately worried, as he shoved her backwards.

'If I can't have you then nobody else can.'

Maggie's knees buckled as she stumbled back, landing on a patch of moss. Looking down at Maggie for a long moment, memories swirling, enraged, he had no choice. Things had gone too far. Leaning closer she could feel his breath on her skin. He'd been drinking, that much was obvious, and when he drank, he always got angry and looked at others to blame for his shit life. He placed his hands on Maggie's throat and tightened his grip on her wildly beating carotid pulse until her eyes bulged and the lights went out.

Dragging her body away from the main path, he covered Maggie with loose vegetation. It would be hours before anyone discovered her if he was lucky. The route was popular with walkers who would hopefully be more interested in the spectacular views than loosely concealed bodies. He brushed Maggie's hair from her face before finally placing a clump of primroses to mask her features. She looked beautiful – dead.

Chapter Seventeen

Maggie Boscawen's body was discovered sometime after lunch by a couple of walkers following the edge of Carrick Roads to St Mawes Castle on this well-known ramblers' route. The husband and wife were on holiday for a week in the fishing village of St Mawes located at the end of this Roseland peninsular. It was the last day of their holiday. The climate in St Mawes was mild all year round and was often described as having its own micro-climate. It was a mecca for the boating and yachting fraternity and geared up for the yuppies.

The middle-aged couple had stopped for a picnic lunch to take in the view across the River Fal towards Falmouth. At first, they saw a mop of hair and then what looked like a pair of jeans. As they inched closer, they could see the woman's green lifeless eyes open, cloudy with a milky-white film of death but no less penetrating. She appeared oddly at peace.

Cornish received the call that a body had been found and along with her team they made their way by car to the nearest parking point before the only accessible walking path to the spot.

Cornish recognised Maggie Boscawen immediately. Cornish would have to call it in. Cornwall Air Ambulance would have to come out and retrieve the body. The coroner's van would collect the dead woman from the helipad landing site in Truro.

The walkers gave their statement to the police and the address where they were staying. Bray happened to find herself on duty that afternoon and having declared Maggie Boscawen dead she notified Gilbert that his next case was on its way.

Turner turned up like a bad penny with her team hoping that not too many people had trampled over her crime scene and sealed off the site. Rain was expected later in the day, and it was essential that any evidence was collected and preserved before it disappeared.

Cornish had no idea what Maggie had been doing on the headland other than taking in the fresh air. They knew nothing about Maggie's life. Cornish was now inquisitive. The deaths were stacking up thick and fast, Lowenna Pascoe, Roger Pascoe and now their daughter Maggie. Cornish thought that if something smelt like shit, then it was shit.

If someone was killing off the family members, there could only be one reason for that – money. A second motive could be power, or control and that could mean someone wanted to own all or the majority of the Pascoe inheritance. Someone was removing any potential obstacles, and they didn't appear to care about the risks. A third possibility was that Maggie Boscawen was killed in a lover's tryst or by her husband. The husband was always the first suspect. The body count was piling up. They had no killer, and no explanation or motive as yet. Cornish persevered with the nagging thoughts in her head and thought we can't always have what we want, can we?

Back at headquarters, the team gathered while Gilbert carried out the post-mortem on Maggie Boscawen.

Cornish started off the discussion.
'What we have on this whiteboard are the names and photographs of those deceased and the ones currently alive, for now, regarding the Pascoe family. On the other display board, I don't need to state the obvious, are the alleged Satanic ritual killings. We are currently assuming there is no correlation between the two boards.

The facts as we know them are Lowenna Pascoe drowned. Or did she? If not, then who stood to gain from her death? We now know Lowenna Pascoe changed her will. Roger was unaware and therefore had a motive to kill his wife if he thought he was next in line. Roger Pascoe was then murdered by someone he possibly knew. The question is why?'

'What about Loveday? ' asked Mac.

'I don't see Roger killing his wife to be with her. He could have walked out years ago if that were the case. Maybe, he was simply fed up with caring for her. The two daughters had a motive, they assumed they were the beneficiaries. The grandchildren allegedly didn't know anything until the reading of her will and Maggie Boscawen appears to have been murdered by strangulation.
What do we know about Strangulation?'

Mac was keen to offer his knowledge of such crimes. 'Strangulation has been recently identified as one of the deadliest forms of domestic violence. I don't think it was a stranger.'

'That's true' replied Cornish 'I don't believe this is a random act of killing. It could be an intimate partner. Are we suggesting the husband or a lover? Did Maggie Boscawen have any marital problems? Was she having an affair? DS Hutchens and DC Mac look into the background of her marriage, and DS Pearce see what else you can find out from the locals. You know that area well. Let's get on with it shall we.'

Cornish knew the press would have a field day if they got hold of the story. Loss of any form was distressing enough but intentional and violent killing brought with it a complicated grieving process that would be interrupted by a police investigation and trivialised in favour of a criminal investigation. Cornish and her team would have to deal with the impact of murder and the sequence of events that brought it about which could re-traumatise the family further. This whole case was getting more sobering, traumatic and messier. The last thing the family would want now is intrusive media coverage, and their names and pictures splashed all over the papers. Their private grief would essentially become public property. The reality of murder was just devastation and sorrow and a time where family supported one and other. Cornish didn't think that was the case with this family.

Cornish made a statement to the press. Jane Falconbridge had insisted they give the media something rather than have them sniffing around all corners grasping at straws and creating their own take on the events. The last thing she wanted was hysteria within the general public.

'The body of Maggie Boscawen was discovered earlier on today on Carrick Roads. It is too early to say how she died. The devastating tragedy will no doubt have a lasting impact on the families concerned and the whole community. We will reveal more information once the forensic experts have completed their investigation.'

A local resident who did not want to be named said 'Mrs Boscawen was hugely respected. Such a death was going to affect the community deeply where all were connected to each other one way or another.'

Cornish wanted to talk to the family and gauge their reaction to Maggie's death. First on the agenda was the husband Steve Boscawen.

Cornish and Pearce arrived at the opulent home of Maggie and Steve Boscawen. They had lived in the parish of St Mawes since their wedding twenty-five years earlier. The vast majority of the high-end properties were now second homes. Effortlessly chic and classy unlike Padstow which was overrun with tourists, St Ives which had now become too cliched and Newquay which was packed with stags, hens and all manner of party-lovers looking for a good time. What you didn't expect to find in St Mawes was a murder in this small and out the way tiny pocket of tranquil modernity with a traditional Cornish heart. Unlike the fishermen's cottages in the heart of the village and fronting the harbour and the narrow streets to the small waterfront moorings, Maggie and Steve's home occupied an enviable position over the Percuil River and surrounding National Trust countryside within a very desirable part of St Mawes.

Pearce whistled at the splendour of Heron House.

'Wow, what a pad. I'd like a piece of what they've got if you don't mind.'

'With a slice of murder on the side?' Cornish quipped.

'When you put it like that, maybe not. It does have its downsides. Never the less, one can admire from afar.'

Steve opened the door and walked back into the kitchen leaving the two police officers to follow. He'd been drinking, that much was obvious. His eyes were bloodshot, Cornish assumed from crying and lack of sleep, and he looked dishevelled. Too many deaths in a short space of time affected everyone.

It was a heart-breaking moment, a husband suddenly losing his wife and in such awful circumstances. The look of concern, and then horror etched on his face as Cornish explained how Maggie had been killed. Cornish and Pearce sat down opposite this broken man and began to question his movements on the day in question. They wanted to know what he did, where he worked and if there were any marital problems slipped into the conversation. Steve robotically answered the questions. He claimed that his marriage had been rock solid protesting his innocence of any wrongdoing in his marriage.

Cornish observed Steve's body language as he spoke and there was an almost imperceptible nod as he said they had never had any problems in the marital department, his body language betraying the truth that his words had worked so hard to hide. His arms were folded, motionless, his face impassive and he was silent when not being asked a question. But Steve couldn't control every movement, a sideways glance or the odd reflex twitch of nervousness. His body language indicated he had something to hide.

Cornish and Pearce took it in turns to offer sympathy with suggestive questions to wrong-foot Steve. He stuck to his story. Steve admitted he had a drinking problem, there was no point in denying that. It was on his medical record, and he was pretty plastered from an earlier drinking session. He hadn't been at work the day Maggie had been killed because of his drinking the night before. There was no point in lying, the police would check out his statement with work. Maggie had taken the dog out for a walk, it wasn't unusual for her to be gone for a couple of hours, so he'd thought nothing of it. He left the house late morning to go and meet a mate at Tehidy Park Golf Club to clear his head. By the time he got back their dog Frank was sitting in the drive and then the police turned up with news of Maggie's death.

Barry turned up just as Cornish and Pearce were leaving. 'I hope you're not accusing my father of my mother's murder. Why don't you go out and find the real killer? We've had to disconnect the phone and cover the windows. The media siege is unbearable.'
Steve intervened.
'They're just doing their job.'
Barry wasn't finished.
'They're going to investigate this, and they're going to find that you are innocent. This is all going to go away like a bad dream.'

The police left Barry and Steve. Inside the house, instead of conversation, there was silence. What had happened was beyond words. Maggie had been Barry's sounding board. She was much stronger than his father, and when, as a younger man, he started having mental health problems, she did everything she could to help him. Even his father was unaware. It had all been dealt with privately and discreetly.

Barry had his own apartment in St Mawes. Steve was relieved when he left. He had always been difficult, demanding, overindulged and an obnoxious child and had consequently grown into an unstable young man who aspired above his intelligence.

Once more alone Steve took out the bottle of vodka and poured himself a stiff drink. He looked in the mirror and cried tears for his Maggie.
'Stevie boy, you should have been an actor.'

Chapter Eighteen

Gilbert was having one hell of a year so far. The busiest he could recall for a long time. More bodies than he could cope with. He'd requested extra hands on deck, and for once his request had been granted by Falconbridge. Two newbies had been sent down from Exeter.

He had insisted on doing Maggie Boscawen's post-mortem alone. He wanted to enjoy spending time with this one to savour her secrets. Gilbert surveyed Maggie Boscawen's body like a hunter, he felt invasive, a voyeur. Maggie Boscawen had a great figure. For a dead woman. It wasn't often that Gilbert felt a stirring, but this woman radiated sexual desire even when dead. Whether it was her classic English rose complexion, now dulled due to death or the greenness of her eyes. He added to his report; Pretty too. He was going to enjoy examining her petite body. He wondered if she'd had a tryst with another man. Had she been asking for it with a body like hers? His job was at the darkest end of the system. He'd seen horrors. And the reality of death was scarier than horror films. He found it interesting that women were far less frightened of blood and pain than men and were drawn to horror and scary movies. He understood why people killed, murdered. It was a profoundly primal act to watch, play out, the things you most fear happening to you.

The gender cliché was there should be more female serial killers. Maybe they were too smart to ever get caught. There was a mistaken cultural assumption that women were incapable of being serial killers. This was a deadly mistake to make, one in six serial killers were female. Their crimes tended to go undetected for longer. The women had an average age of 32 for their first killing and poison was the most common method. A female killer would kill for financial gain, lust or thrill or power.

Cornish had guessed Maggie Boscawen had been strangled from the contusions on her neck. Listening to Gilbert relay his examination she was puzzled.

'Her body exhibited post-mortem hypostasis from lying on her back. The blood had accumulated on her underside for the several hours' post-death and the fact that it was cold and exposed to the weather. She was perfect apart from the fact that her voice box was swollen and the right cornua of her hyoid bone in her neck had been dislocated. There had been some regurgitation of food found in her sound box. Her neck was broken. She had been strangled to death by relatively small hands, but that's no indication of this being a woman. In my opinion, this was a man with small hands.'

He laughed at his own joke.

'You know small hands and feet, small dick.'

Cornish raised her eyes to the ceiling and muttered 'so help me God' before looking back at Gilbert who continued.

'Maggie Boscawen was murdered.'

Cornish ignored Gilbert's typically tactless jibe. She'd heard plenty of them over the years, but he always managed to surprise her with something new. You had to be special to work in this particular area of science. It wasn't for the faint-hearted. For one thing, Cornish could never get used to the flickering lights when examining a dead body, yet it seemed to happen frequently.

'Gilbert, to clarify, in your professional opinion was this murder carried out by a male or female?'

'Strangulation is almost always men and the victims almost always women. That isn't to say a woman couldn't strangle another woman. Maggie Boscawen was slight, and the murderer had, as I said, small hands. Her death would have been quick if that's any consolation to the family. Her body wasn't moved, she was strangled at that site and covered over with foliage. She had been dead for approximately three hours before her body was discovered. Maggie Boscawen died that Friday morning, 15 March around 10 am.

Cornish decided it was time to interview the rest of the family and she hoped that Pearce had found out further useful information that may lead them to the killer. What concerned and focused her mind was the significance of the date or someone's idea of a sick joke murdering

Maggie Boscawen on the Eides of March.

Chapter Nineteen

Nadine Pascoe lived in Truro. She enjoyed city life. Living in the countryside was dull, boring and stank. She'd been brought up on Lankelly Farm and wasn't sorry to see the back of farm life and her father. And as soon as she could, she persuaded her mother to let her take over the Lemon Street property. An elegant Georgian house with well-proportioned accommodation suitable for a growing family. It was also closer to Maggie via the King Harry ferry.

Nadine was devastated by Maggie's death.
'There is something wrong with a person who could do this, and you think it could be one of us? That someone capable of murder could emerge from our family?'

Cornish was accompanied by Hutchens. They probed Nadine for information. Divorced, she was continuously embroiled in her own bitter battles with Eddy Hicks, a notorious womaniser and rogue tradesman. Nadine had reverted back to her maiden name of Pascoe. She didn't have a kind word to say about her ex-husband. He wouldn't ever see a penny of her family's inheritance. Guilt was eating away at her, and she was relieved to finally get what she wanted to say off her chest.

'Barry wasn't Steve's son. Maggie wouldn't say who the father was. She lost a daughter before she had Barry, she's buried at St Just in Roseland church. I would usually meet her there on the anniversary of her daughter's death but didn't go this time because of this stupid quarrel.

I didn't get to say goodbye as her sudden death happened so fast. And I miss her every day. Maybe if I had met her, she would still be alive.'

Cornish didn't think so.

Nadine owned the Truro house and had an income from the family business. She didn't need to be involved in the day to day running anymore and left it up to her children Emma and Paul. Emma was the eldest by two years at 32 and lived in an apartment in Truro near to her mother.

As Nadine closed the door, she looked at herself in the mirror. She'd aged overnight. She'd told the police enough. Somethings were better staying buried in the past where they belonged.

Chapter Twenty

Cornish and Hutchens were surprised at Emma's coldness. 'My mother lived in her sister's shadow. When Maggie said jump my mother jumped? Maggie could be a prize bitch when it suited her. My mother was never good enough compared to her. Her husband Steve is a jack ass. All mouth and no trousers. Acts like the big man but the reality is he's a pathetic loser. Maggie married him so she could be the boss. Not the other way around.
As for Barry, he's just a greedy bastard child. Not Steve's son, in case you hadn't heard.'

Cornish raised her eyebrows as the fountain of information poured out of Emma. She was an angry young woman. Was she enraged enough to commit murder?

Emma was on a roll, happy to discuss her family's wealth. She dealt with the administrative aspects of the family business, had a great lifestyle and no boyfriend on the horizon.

'I'm not gay by the way. I swing both ways. It's more fun like that. I'm not with anyone at the moment.'

Whether Emma liked to employ shock tactics, Cornish couldn't work her out.

As they left the apartment, Cornish turned to Hutchens.

'I got the feeling she fancied you.'

'Not my type ma'am.'

They laughed as they got into Cornish's camper and drove off.

Emma watched from her window as the two police officers left in the strange vehicle of choice. She had landed on her feet. Emma was cool under a crisis. She should have been more charming, but it was too late for that. Still, she had given them the information to disarm them and divert the attention away from herself. Forensic evidence was fragile at best and didn't last forever, destroyed by weather, the environment, the perpetrator and even wild animals.

Emma had sleeping problems her whole life. The funny thing about going to the doctor was that if you tell them you've had sleeping problems, they just hand you a leaflet. That's how Emma discovered she was interested in serial killers and death. Drinking, smoking and watching late night TV Emma would watch CSI, crime documentaries and cold cases before moving on to buying DVDs about serial killers. Eventually, her doctor prescribed sleeping tablets. The tablets would take an hour to kick in, but old habits die hard, and she was hooked on macabre and violence. She learnt all the ways a person could get caught and a list of things to know if the desire was there to kill someone.

Emma knew she was a suspect. She would have been disappointed if she weren't. After all, she had reasons for wanting her family dead, even if the police were unaware of them. If they were any good at their job, they would undoubtedly find out.

Yes, she had plenty of reasons if the truth was known. There was a lot of money at stake, millions. That was always a good start. Then there was revenge. Her grandfather had abused his daughters and then Paul and herself. Revenge murder had a great sound to it. Emma knew if it were revenge she wanted then she would only get one chance of getting away with murder. Each time she murdered after that she rolled the dice, and her chances of getting caught would be higher. Emma recognised that it was so much more pleasurable to kill someone she knew and not a random stranger. And, she enjoyed the odd game of craps.

Then there would be the evidence. The police had no evidence to place Emma at the scene of any of the recent murders; otherwise, she would be in an interview room in the police station under caution. That is assuming she had killed anybody in the first place. Now that was an interesting thought to ponder.

Emma knew from her DVDs that if she were the killer and tried to eliminate the evidence, then that would most likely create more evidence.

The old adage of don't kill the person you're sleeping with would make you the prime suspect. That always ended badly. Like a spurned lover she had taken her revenge and sod the consequences.

The fewer people that were aware of your proclivities, the better. Better still, tell no one. You may have to kill them later else. Always commit the murder yourself, don't hire someone. You could become a blackmail target, and that wouldn't do.

Emma recognised an intelligent being when she met one. Cornish had the measure of most people. But the police were overstretched continuously and overworked. Murder cases were built on progress and like everything else had a budget. No progress and no chance of progress and all dead ends would make the police move on to the next case quickly. Give the cops constant dead ends and wrap them up in different directions. Confuse the hell out of them. Murder was something you carried around with you for life. Emma was an expert at compartmentalising her life. Murder was wrong and messy. Everyone knew murder was a sin. 'Vengeance is mine' sayeth the Lord. Emma knew that getting away with murder was difficult. But not impossible.

Chapter Twenty-One

Cornish and Hutchens drove across to the other side of Cornwall to the north coast. Paul Hicks lived in Padstow, Padstein to the locals. At the head of the Camel River, this quaint working fishing port was surrounded by glorious sandy beaches.

Paul was an even colder fish than Emma when he first opened the door viewing the police with suspicion. Then it was as if someone had flicked a switch and he turned into charming personified. Cornish and Hutchens took it in turns to ask leading questions to Paul. Where was he on specific dates, what did he do and who did he see? Paul showed no remorse for the deaths of his grandparents and no empathy for the way Maggie had died.

'She deserved what she got as far as I'm concerned, and no I didn't kill her? I didn't need to kill her. You should be looking at Barry if you ask me. Or her pathetic browbeaten husband.'

Paul was in charge of organising the repairs and upkeep of the family properties and land, only he mainly surfed when he could, which was most of the time and did his own thing. He had always lived on the fringes of society, and he liked it that way.

'I don't have a current girlfriend, but if I want one, then I just take my pick. They're all gagging for it around here.'

Cornish asked the loaded question.

Have you been out with anyone lately?

'No, I haven't had much time what with all the deaths and funerals. They've kind of kept me somewhat preoccupied.'

A smart ass to boot.

'Any good pubs around here?' enquired Hutchens.

'You could try the Fishermans Arms in St Merryn, Padstow suggested Paul.

'Is there anything else we should know or be aware of that you could possibly help us with Paul?'

Cornish was trying to delve beneath the surface for the real Paul. With stone cold killers she had learned that underneath the many layers of violent and sociopathic tendencies there was usually a person who simply needed help. Flattery in interviews was a favourite technique employed.

'I cry myself to sleep most nights.'

A glimmer of humanity had seeped into the conversation. Cornish responded.

'Do you know why?'

'Yes, it took Emma and me many years to come to terms with what our grandfather did to us. He abused us as children. Didn't Emma mention it? It's not something you forget. But that doesn't mean I killed my grandparents.'

Paul was calm, not angry. He exhibited no rage as Cornish carefully asked.

'Would you like to have killed your grandfather?'

'Of course, but that would be wrong. I know my grandfather loved me in his own way.'

Cornish and Hutchens observed his clenched hands as he spoke trying to convey his strained words with love, concern and empathy for his grandfather. She wasn't convinced.

'Thank you for being so open and honest with us.'

Paul watched as the two women drove off.

He didn't trust these two bitches. The police lied as far as he was concerned, and they viewed him as a suspect. He'd been careful. Emma had a plan. She would appreciate the way he let that piece of information slip out. Confuse the hell out of the police.

Chapter Twenty-Two

Cornish had got what she came for, and she and Hutchens thanked Paul Hicks for his time. She informed him she would be at Maggie Boscawen's funeral.

Cornish was the first to speak when they got in the Camper.

'That was an interesting conversation? Don't you think? A rather sarcastic and curt individual. Both he and Emma were abused by Roger Pascoe which gives them a motive. Paul Hicks hated Maggie Boscawen with a passion and that gives him a motive. And he knows the Fishermans Arms. Was he there the night in question that Derwa was there? Paul Hicks may well be a sociopath.'

Hutchens agreed, nodding as she drove.
'I bet he was a right little shit at public school.'

Cornish pulled into the Fishermans Arms. They were technically off duty for the night. There was one more question to ask.

Cornish approached the landlord.

'Any chance of a bite to eat. Your pub was recommended to us by Paul Hicks?'

'Yes, Take a seat. Paul's a regular here. I'll bring over the menus.'

That was easy.

As they sat down with their wine and food, they dissected their earlier conversation with Paul Hicks.

'Hutchens, as we know most antisocial personalities are learned, usually through an abusive or neglected childhood. Both Emma and Paul were abused. You noticed that both siblings were pretty callous about their family and not convincing with their charm. They both lack empathy for the murders and deaths. Unlike their mother Nadine who was really cut up. She managed to have two children who are emotionally empty.

Maybe she spoilt them as children, missed or ignored the abuse, and the result is two adults that haven't grown up.

They are essentially both immature, selfish, self-centred, resentful with the raging child from the sexual abuse inside the adult body. They could be extremely dangerous people.'

'Where does that leave us with this case?' Hutchens asked.

'We have several family members who have a motive for murder. Everyone has something in their closet that they want to keep hidden. Maggie Boscawen has one son Barry, a daughter buried, and Steve Boscawen is not the biological father of Barry. Does Steve Know? Does Barry know? The daughter that's buried. How did she die? Who is her father? Was Maggie Boscawen having an affair? We still need answers.

It isn't evil that drives people to kill. They are driven by devastating histories of trauma. Interestingly, rich people fall into the emotional void category. The pursuit of money fills the need for love and human affection. Money makes people, even rich people, do crazy things.

Serial killers are usually on some sort of power trip, and they enjoy watching their victims suffer through torture. It's not usually lust, more of a god complex.'

Cornish and Hutchens pondered over the case as they ate. There was no such thing as a senseless killing.
Each crime had its own logic. Even if the outside world couldn't see it.

Chapter Twenty-Three

Finley Jago had driven his crappy heap of a car to Hell's Mouth, near Hayle. He'd lived in Hayle all his life and had always had high aspirations, but the reality of his life was that he'd never escape his background or his lack of intelligence. He was in a dead-end job, and his future looked bleak. His mother was a manic depressive and his father a jobless drunk. The only one to have got out and try to make something of themselves was his older brother who had joined the army. Instead, he'd come back in a box and was now buried in the crematorium. Some families simply never had any luck, no matter how hard they tried, and Finley was now convinced his family were cursed with the same misfortune. Why fight what was surely fate and meant to be.

The steep cliff face was a renowned spot for committing suicide with its dramatic 300 ft drop. He'd walked the coast path over the years with his mates. There was now a fancy café at the top of the cliffs and tourists flocked to try and catch a glimpse of the seals. He now stood looking out to sea contemplating his death. No one would miss him. He intended to jump, but as he looked down over the beach to the children playing in the sand and the surfers, he realised he hadn't even got the nerve to do that. He was a pathetic waste of space. There were too many people around enjoying their Easter break. Instead, Finley drove to Godrevy to watch the surfers ride the waves and rethink his future.

Godrevy had a reputation for soft breaking waves and being suitable for learner surfers. Today the swell was over 4 ft, and the wind was anything other than perfect. The surfers were struggling to paddle out and ride the waves back in towards the sandy beach. Finley envied them. They were confident, one moment they were riding the crest of a wave, unbeatable and exuding unbelievable self-belief, and the next they were thrown off their boards, out of control and caught in the sea's grip. And yet, they still got back on their boards and tried again. Confidence was a funny thing, and Finley envied the surfers battling against the elements. He couldn't even swim.

He sat and watched them ride out and roll back in on the white horses. One of the saddest things in the world was to feel broken. He felt ripped apart by his brother's death and didn't think he could ever be put back together again. A part of him had been taken away forever. At least his brother had made something of his short life. There were days when Finley asked himself what was he staying here for? Most days he didn't have the answer. Today was one of those days, a tough day being the anniversary of his bro's death. His depression was overwhelming. He had reached rock bottom and couldn't see any way out.

He didn't notice the figure approaching him carrying his surfboard until he sat down beside him and plonked his board on the sand.

'Hey, dude! Surf's evolving today. Waves are bowling hard. I got plenty of speed, but the whole thing closed out behind me. It was sick, you know what I'm saying.'

It was like listening to a foreign language. Finley looked out at the surfer and spoke.

'Not me man. I've come out today to top myself.'

'You don't want to do that. It scars those you leave behind. You don't want to damage your family permanently by topping yourself. Nah, come with me. Let's have some fun, we'll catch a few bevvies and put the world to rights.'

Finley felt better speaking to a stranger. His mates wouldn't have understood, but this guy got him.

'Leave your car, we'll go in mine.'

Finley got into the Range Rover and sat surrounded by surfing gear. This rich guy lived for the sea and the surf. Maybe his luck was turning.

They drove for ages along the coast road amiably chatting about this and that. Finley didn't feel alone. This stranger was rapidly becoming a friend. Talking to him loosened the tangled monster that gripped him and was still a tangle inside, but for once Finley felt he was willing to let go and release this darkness to navigate into safer waters of friendship. He suddenly felt embarrassed to think he had been going to meet his maker earlier, but this guy sitting next to him wasn't making anything of it and distancing himself from him, unlike his so-called mates.

The car pulled into the car park of the Star Inn in the Cornish town of St Just in Penwith. The old inn was built of granite and had been associated with the tin mining industry and the sea. The slate-covered floors were well trodden and the pub timeless and friendly. The locals acknowledged his friend, they knew him and readily accepted Finley into the fold. It was a proper old-fashioned Cornish pub, convivial company and good beer which is what this pub was known for. No food and no frills and an old-school barman who chatted to all his customers. So very Cornish Finley could imagine the smugglers in their droves in this fine hostelry.

Finley's companion was busy jostling with others in the pub. Finley sat and listened enraptured by the easy banter and whit of the company. It was dark and last orders had been rung by the bell by the time his friend suggested that they head back. They had consumed copious amounts of beer and Finley was three sheets to the wind, pissed without a care in the world. He hadn't noticed his last pint had an additional ingredient added. Finley sat in the passenger seat of the Range Rover and closed his eyes suddenly weary as the sedative started to take effect. He felt groggy and relaxed to the point of not having a care in the world.

The five-holed stones found on Kenidjack Common were considered somewhat of an enigma. The stones formed a row of four, three of which were holed with a further stone broken that sat outside the main alignment. The hourglass profile of the holes dated back to the Bronze Age and on stormy nights the sound phenomena were hauntingly mysterious. The arrangements of the stones were said to have Devil worshipping properties and were orientated to marry the solar and lunar calendars for releasing hidden powers through ceremonial rituals. Tonight, was Good Friday and the Day of Passion and the Death of Christ for which human male sacrifice was required. The group would be pleased with his choice.

Finley aided by his companion managed to walk the short distance from the remote car park to the stones. Torches had been set at intervals to illuminate the rocks, and there appeared to be others gathered wearing black robes with hoods. Finley could see their nakedness underneath as they welcomed him into their circle and removed his clothes. He didn't resist as they gently spoke, their melodic voices drawing him closer. He was laid down on a flat granite rock within the alignment, and his limbs were outstretched and restrained rather like pitching a tent with its pegs.
He felt somewhat self-conscious yet sexually uninhibited as tongues, mouths and hands encased his growing erection. The ritual had commenced. The leader of the Satanic group was his friend who smiled at him as he lay there naked as a new-born baby. But, as Finley looked into his eyes, he could see the soulless eyes of the devil. Recanting words as a form of true self-love their leader spoke.

'With our sacrifice tonight, we are destroying stupid things and making ourselves stronger and lighter and more powerful. We have removed our material clothes and our possessions to do this to embrace our culture. Our social status and self-worth are assigned by what we have, and this sacrifice will bring us further that which we desire. This sacrifice tonight is noxious and deserving. This individual sought to destroy himself through self-destruction, and we must eliminate such emotional leeches dragging others down. Actions have consequences, and this bad behaviour must be subjugated. As the eleventh ruler of the Eleven Satanic Rules of the Earth states: when walking in open territory, bother no one. If someone bothers you and does not stop, then you must destroy him. The beast does not want a material offering but a soul.'

Finley stared into the eyes of this man he had just met and saw nothing except loathing and hatred. Gone was the amiable character of earlier. This man was a monster who had preyed on his lost soul. Finley realised at that moment that he had no luck and would never have any. His family were destined to be miserable their whole lives, and his life had just got shorter. This sacrifice would be an end to it, and as he looked into the eyes of hell, he could only mutter two words.

'Thank you.'

Using the serrated hunting knife, Finley's throat was slit before his genitals were skilfully removed and the rest of his organs. All of his teeth were then plucked out and his eyes removed before finally washing in Finley's blood. Lastly, his dead body was hacked up into pieces to be disposed of. There would be no evidence for anyone to suspect a satanic ritual had taken place this time. They had learnt their lesson. If they wished to continue their practices, then they needed to be more careful. They scattered as quietly as they had arrived, the two women in one car and the two men separately. Their leader watched the men drive away and realised they would have to be dealt with soon. They weren't family and that in itself was a problem. Nevertheless, five could keep a secret if four of them were dead.

Chapter Twenty-Four

Cornish and her team hadn't had a day off since the start of the spate of deaths to hit Cornwall. They had all been on double shifts and were worn out. Jane Falconbridge considered it a pointless task to flog her staff to death and instructed them to at least take some time over the Easter break to recharge their batteries. All appeared quiet on the major crime front apart from the apparent multiple murders. Maggie Boscawen's funeral had been delayed, and no other bodies had been found, or anyone reported missing so far. Cornish wasn't convinced that the killings had stopped. She had the unshakable feeling that the latest murder had yet to be discovered.

The Anchor Inn was a popular drinking hole for Cornish and her team and within easy reach of Bodmin Headquarters. They gathered in the back room for a beer and a basket of good pub grub, something with triple cooked chips. None of them had anybody at home to go back to.

Pearce was divorced, his wife hadn't considered she would be married to the force and eventually left him for a local solicitor. Pearce couldn't blame her as he was never at home and when he was there physically, his mind was elsewhere.

Hutchens was renting a place which still looked as if she had just moved in yesterday. Boxes had yet to be unpacked, and the fridge was devoid of food.

Mac had moved back home and was saving up a deposit for his own place. Until then he was relying on his parent's goodwill, and as the youngest of his siblings living at home, he was waited on by his doting older mother and father who didn't understand his need for putting himself in the firing line every day.

Cornish nursed a large glass of wine as the conversation shifted from the Pascoe murders to the Satanic cult rituals. None of them had any outside hobbies to speak of and would probably end up twitching their thumbs all weekend.

Englebert sat patiently waiting for any titbits to come his way. He spent most of his days in the Camper Van watching the world of crime pass him by. He had become the team's good luck mascot, and colleagues were used to him wandering around Headquarters where he had his own basket and bowl. Most of the time though he was on the road with Claire.

Cornish dropped off Hutchens on the way home. She had no intention of doing anything other than spending her time off, in bed and taking Englebert for walks, weather permitting.

Cornish listened intently to the wind as she lay in bed with a well-earned cup of tea, a rare treat on a Saturday morning. The wind carried the scent of the sea through the open sash window, and she loved the noise as it whipped around the corners of her cottage. The sea from her window view was choppy with plenty of white horses to keep the leisure boats in the harbour moored up. At least the harbour master would have a quiet day providing some idiot visitor didn't decide to be gung-ho and take a boat out.

By early morning Claire and Englebert were walking the path from Ready Money Cove through the National Trust woods to St Catherine's Castle. There she and Englebert perched to admire the spectacular vista out and over the river. The rain which had been threatening had held off. She never tired of the view and always found this a place of solace to think over her life and decisions she had made in the past, for better or for worse. Claire had walked the complete circular walk many times which stretched from Fowey to Polkerris and then back along the Saints Way, an ancient long-distance footpath. The Saints Way was a 27-mile route in total across Cornwall from Fowey on the south coast to Padstow, but in all honesty, Claire hadn't got the staying power to complete it anymore, or the desire, and definitely not the time.

Claire and Englebert sat side by side enjoying the solitude. For once Claire felt in touch with the land she knew and acknowledged in her heart that she would never leave for anywhere else. They will have to carry me away in a box from here Claire thought, even then, she had made her wishes clear that she wanted her ashes to be scattered from this very spot. Claire was Cornish through and through, and that would never change. Her thoughts lingered as she stroked her faithful companion. He was her baby now.

By the time Claire walked through her front door she was ready for a fry up of the works, bacon, sausage, fried egg, mushroom and tomatoes and a mug of tea. The rest of the day she intended to spend catching up and watching soaps on TV, and any other reality shows that she had missed. She found it intriguing that people were so willing to make complete fools of themselves in front of millions of strangers for money. It was her way of switching off her brain from her normal everyday hectic life, watching some idiot with fake boobs and botoxed to the hilt prattle on about how hard her life was. There was no denying the contestants weren't exactly University Challenge material, but the programme operated on many levels to create theatre and pander to its intelligent viewers. With its clever editing and the simple relaying of conversations, even the GCSE students would snigger at the ineptitude of the participants. Claire had nothing else to do. From a feminist point of view, all the men treated the women terribly referring to some as slags on the air for all to see. It was your basic junk TV with sexy people. That was the secret to its success.

Claire lounged on her settee until Englebert started to get restless. He was a creature of habit and demanded his tea at 4.30 pm on the dot. Claire walked him across to Ready Money Cove, and she watched him dig holes refilling the previous hole with the new sand before they finally traipsed back indoors.

Claire's meal of choice for dinner was a Marks and Spencer spaghetti bolognaise in the 'meal for two' range with dessert and a bottle of red wine. Settled on the sofa, she intended to binge watch her favourite show CSI. Gilbert had informed her during one of the many autopsies she had observed that watching episode after episode of a show was good for you, it made you feel good and released the chemical dopamine in your brain giving the body a natural, internal reward of pleasure reinforcing the continued engagement in that activity. You, therefore, kept watching while your brain produced a drug-like high. In return, you developed a pseudo-addiction to that particular show because you craved the dopamine release. Gilbert went on further to explain that these same pathways caused other addictions, the body did not discriminate against pleasure. Claire knew what he was instantly referring to – sex. Gilbert had a crush on her.

By the end of the evening, Claire wanted the phone to ring. She'd enjoyed her day wasting time watching mostly inane rubbish, but she couldn't imagine doing it day in and out every day. The TV was a chosen substitute for real life. She sat in bed going over her notes on the cases. No algorithms were going to catch these killers. They weren't a statistic to enter into a machine which would then map out a list of potential suspects. Cornwall didn't see mass murders on this scale every day, and indeed these backwaters didn't possess CCTV scattered everywhere. That was limited to the local town centres and areas of commerce and in bigger towns and cities, not Cornwall. These crimes would be solved manually and by her officers. Claire believed in the law, and her devotion had cost her several relationships, although if she were honest, she never really gave anyone a chance to get close to her.

Cornish knew one thing with absolute certainty.
There was a group of Satanists who would never stop, not so long as self-interest and greed gave them the power they craved.
And the vast majority of killers didn't want to get caught. They loved the act of killing and the satisfaction it gave them. The more they killed, the more confident they became and more experienced. Murder required meticulous planning and disposing of the body.

Cornish believed the killer, or killers relished their ability to murder and avoid detection which was empowering and increasing their excitement to take more risks thinking that they wouldn't get caught. And taking unnecessary risks leads to mistakes. Whatever the reward was for their actions Cornish intended to put a stop to it. Well, we can't always have what we want, can we?

Chapter Twenty-Five

A glorious Easter sunshine dazzled through Claire's bedroom window. The sunbathers would be out in force with their barbeques, pasties and sand sandwiches on Readymoney Beach. Fowey would be jam-packed with tourists, and the boats would be day tripping out on the calm sea.

Claire glanced at her watch and contemplated her Sunday. It wasn't even eight o'clock. Sundays were supposed to be slumberous days of rest yet through years of training she couldn't relax. Breakfast on her front terrace and reading her notes on her lounger watching the world go by sounded good. She had never managed to start a book and finish it, so why bother now. Work was her life. That was about as far as she would get. The shrill sound of the telephone interrupted her plans, and she knew before she even answered the call that she would have to shelve her schedule.

'Cornish.'

Jane Falconbridge never slept, never rested and never took a day off. The whole team were from this moment back on duty.

'A young man by the name of Finley Jago has not returned home. He went out on Friday morning and has not been seen since. His mother made the call to the police this morning. It's unlike her son, not that he was a saint, far from it. Her words were that he could be difficult and a little shit. And he's been having a tough time of it lately. His brother was killed overseas in the army, and he hasn't taken his death well. He drives an old VW Polo, red, the year 2001 three-door, one-litre model.' Falconbridge gave the registration number to Cornish.

'It may be something or nothing, but it wouldn't hurt to see if the vehicle has been found or reported anywhere. None of Finley's mates have seen him.'

'I'll call the team in Ma'am.'

By the time Cornish arrived at Bodmin Headquarters the team were assembled and waiting for their instructions. By some fortuitous luck, the duty sergeant on the desk had received a call from Godrevy Café. The owner had reported a vehicle matching the description as abandoned in the National Trust car park.

'Pearce and Mac, get yourselves down there pronto. Let's see if anybody saw this lad hanging around on Friday along the beach. It's a long beach and connects to Gwithian beach at low tide. The beach attracts surfers, and we know there is no lifeguard on duty until May on Peter's Point. Pick up a photograph from the lad's home on your way there. I'll let the parents know to expect you.'

Pearce and Mac pulled into the rough council estate in Hayle. This particular estate was one of the worse areas in Cornwall and designated a high crime rate area for the county, nowhere near the rest of the country, but for Cornwall, it kept Cornish and her team regularly busy. Arson and theft were the highest offences followed by assaults, murders were rare. This spate of killings had rattled even the hardened criminals and rougher neighbourhoods in the community.

Finley Jago lived in a terraced council estate with rubbish left strewn in the overgrown front gardens and cars hitched up on the road with their wheels missing – stolen. Nobody would have reported the theft for fear of any retaliation. They would have naturally found another vehicle at some point with tyres to suit their car and nabbed them. The prospect of being brought up in this neighbourhood was a depressing thought as Pearce and Mac walked past some snotty nosed toddlers playing unsupervised on the pavement. No one cared.

Mrs Jago opened the front door to let the pigs in as they were known locally. Walking through the untidy hallway, they were shown into the lounge where Jago senior had his arse parked and could be seen through a film of smoke. There was nothing homely about the place, and Pearce could understand why the boy would want to top himself living in this shit hole. Still, they weren't here to judge their standards of cleanliness or how they lived their lives, just to collect a picture of the lad and, hopefully, bring him back home to this dump thought Pearce.

They stood in the lounge waiting for Mrs Jago to find a picture of Finley. The décor looked tired, cheap wallpaper peeled off the walls in places, and the inexpensive round paper lantern shade reminded him of a Chinese restaurant. Everything was shoddy, dirty and tacky. Pearce suspected that old man Jago hadn't done a day's work in his life.

Jago senior had a foul mouth at the best of times, and he observed the two police officers.

'They allow poofters in the force now, do they?'

Pearce watched Mac waiting for a reaction. And this wasn't Mac's first experience of homophobia. He intervened.

'And a bloody good copper looking for your boy.'

Jago senior wasn't used to someone standing up to him, and it blindsided him. He'd lost one son and didn't want to lose his only heir.

'Sorry son. I meant no harm in saying it' was directed at Mac.

An apology from Jago senior coughing and spluttering up his guts was a rare event.

Pearce didn't mention that Finley's car had been found. Once they had the facts, they would update the parents. The police weren't liked in the area, and they didn't want to give the parents any reason to stir up the community.

Mac and Pearce left with a picture of Finley taken when he was at school. They didn't look as if they possessed a camera hence the school picture which was no doubt free and their only one. They would make sure it was returned to them at the end.

The squad car drove out of the estate before Mac spoke up.
'Thanks for that vote of confidence back there.'
'No problem. You're the first gay officer I've worked with. And you're a good cop and should be treated the same as all the other good cops. I guess I'm saying you are ok, lad, to work with. If I had a son like you, I would be proud as hell.'

Mac beamed. A compliment like that was a rarity from Pearce. Mac smiled. Pearce wasn't all hard-nosed and was starting to accept him as a police officer and not a fag as he had previously caught earshot of when he first arrived. They both had to learn how to work together and get along, and he had a feeling that Cornish had deliberately paired them together. Her plan was working.

Cornish and Hutchens were at Godrevy Café when Pearce and Mac walked in. She handed the picture to the café owner who confirmed that Finley had been hanging around. She didn't see where he went.

Cornish didn't have a good feeling about the missing lad.

'Let's walk the beach. Talk to anyone and find out if Paul Hicks and Finley Jago were on the beach on Friday. Speak to all the surfers. Someone must know something.'

Pearce and Mac walked one direction while Cornish and Hutchens took the opposite. The beach was busy for Easter Sunday, and at low tide, three miles of golden sand stretched from Hayle around the bay to Godrevy Cove. There was plenty of space to lose a body. Dogs were allowed on this particular beach which made it all the more attractive for visitors, not so useful for preserving a crime scene.

Cornish didn't think Finley had come all this way to take in the beautiful heathland of the Knavocks. Dramatic Hell's Mouth was well known for jumpers.

The team rendezvoused back at Godrevy Café.

Pearce and Mac had spoken to a couple of surfers.

'Finley was sitting on the beach at first on his own and then with another person, a surfer. They'd seen the surfer guy around before, a regular, not your average dude was how they described him. Well spoken, obviously educated at private school according to these guys. He drives a white Range Rover. They didn't see them go off together. No one else saw anything, Ma'am.'

'Who do we know that drives a Range Rover? Check out what vehicle Paul Hicks drives. He likes surfing. His mobile phone should provide a few answers. And Finley Jago's mobile.'

Cornish rang Jane Falconbridge to authorise the access. The Police forces in England and Wales had come in for a lot of stick recently for extracting data from phones. Privacy International had been calling for this rollout practice to be used under a warrant which just wasn't practical. They wanted the public protected from this Freedom of Information giving the police the power and technology to extract location data, conversations on encrypted apps, call logs, emails, text messages, passwords, internet searches and downloaded deleted data and quickly.

'Current legislation allows us to still access the data where there are reasonable grounds if we believe it to contain evidence in relation to an offence and only then in adherence with data protection and human rights obligations. The government is clear that all police powers must be necessary, proportionate and lawful.'

Falconbridge was a stickler for the rule book.

'I agree Ma'am. I believe I can pinpoint Finley's whereabouts and find him. I also want to look at Paul Hicks phone data. Cornish wanted to find a link.'

Back at Bodmin Headquarters Cornish looked in on the technical department tracing the phones' locations. The IT man in charge was known as Cave Dave. He spent his whole life on a computer. What he didn't know about data in the ether wasn't worth knowing.

'Using cells takes seconds. It doesn't matter if you're calling the other side of the world. When any mobile phone access cell's your IMEI is transmitted and tracked. It doesn't matter if you change your SIM card number, it's the phones IMEI number that is tracked. Hence the reason why people buy a cheap phone and discard it away after a crime or steal someone else's to avoid detection. The actual time taken to track a mobile phone device is two seconds. You can track it using one cell for a general location, with two cells you get an exact location. With three cells you get triangulation, the most accurate.'

'What have you discovered' enquired Cornish.

'Well, Finley Jago's phone is dead. It's switched off, so I can't place any trace, not without the phone. Either that or he never had a phone, highly unlike given the generation today. That's the bad news. Paul Hicks phone is alive and working and shows him on Polzeath Beach currently. On Friday he was on Godrevy Beach. And Friday evening, he was in the Star Inn in the Cornish town of St Just in Penwith.'

'You've just made my day Dave. I could kiss you.'
Cornish left a red-faced Dave.

Hutchens, Pearce and Mac were beaming when she walked in the room.
'You'll never guess who drives a white Range Rover' Pearce announced.

'Paul Hicks' replied Cornish.
'Pearce and Mac get down to the Star Inn with Finley's picture. We've had disappearances over the years, but I

think this young man was picked up by Paul Hicks and driven somewhere nearby the Star Inn and possibly killed. Hutchens and I will follow.

I want to look at somewhere first where the Devil rides a black horse and mortals must run to escape his grasp.'

Chapter Twenty-Six

Cornish zoomed along the Cornish lanes expecting that at any moment she would come face to face with an oncoming SUV or a trundling tractor. Hutchens gripped the sides of her seat as she thought the winding lanes would have necessitated a slower pace. The retro van looked antiquated but was far from it. For all its foibles and difficult driving Cornish loved her vintage camper and putting it through its paces.

They were heading down to Penwith, the wild at heart and isolated moorland near the Star Inn. Even at Easter, it looked macabre and spine-chilling. A reflection of the wildness of this stretch of moorland. The area was a funerary landscape, dotted with tumuli, Cairns and quoits, as they were known in Cornwall. This area was known for its supernatural entities according to folklore information that Cornish had discovered on the internet. References to the piskie belief were all over Cornwall but here between

Pendeen and St just, at Carn Kenidjack and Woon Gumpus Common, the folklore took a sinister turn.

When Cornish heard that Paul Hicks was in Penwith something clicked into place. She wanted to see Kenidjack Common for herself. She parked her camper in the grassed National Trust carpark where Paul Hicks had parked on Friday. Cornish and Hutchens were the only ones in the car park. Hutchens noticed the tyre tracks.

'Someone's been here recently looking at the marks. Possibly our Range Rover?'

'Maybe' replied Cornish. 'I don't like this place. It feels wrong. Can you feel it?'

There was a feeling of foreboding in the air, a glumness and macabre depression. It felt a sad, unforgiving place. The message was very clear, though the mechanism by which Cornish sensed it was a mystery. She felt as if she was being warned of the hilltop. This land suddenly felt incredibly powerful and sinister. Something evil lurked in the wind. Yet as compelling as it seemed to run away Cornish stood transfixed. There was no going back.

Hutchens observed the fear in Cornish and felt her hackles rise. They had to go forward if they were to find out what happened. They trudged towards the stones. These weren't healing stones but stones that had been part of Satanic and barbaric rituals. The sounds emanating from the hollows were like whispers as if the stones were communicating with each other. This place was a dwelling of souls and spirits. Murmuring and whispering sounds filled the air, except there was no one beside you.

A cursed place and full of evil souls. Visiting this site confirmed in Cornish's mind that evil did exist. There was a presence of souls and spirits here in Cornwall. It was dusk as they reached the stones. Cornish and Hutchens surveyed the site, they saw nothing untoward yet underneath the ground was Satan's invisible cemetery if the Satanic cult were to be believed. Evidence of that would fade over time as the earth engulfed the sacrifices. Cornish and Hutchens could see no evidence of a recent burial. Cornish studied the ground. It looked rich and discoloured, and as she touched the soil, it felt sticky.

'Hutchens, I think this is blood. Look at the area. It's everywhere if I'm not mistaken. Someone bled out here.'

Cornish and Hutchens walked the stones. Sure, enough someone or something had been slaughtered on this very spot.

'Call Lucy Turner. Get SOCO out here. This is now an official crime scene.'

Two hours later a full team had cordoned off the area and soil samples taken. Somebody now had the task of matching the DNA found in this blood with Finley Jago. Cornish would call in to see the parents and get something with Finley's DNA. Alternatively, the parents could be matched as Turner explained.

'In the absence of a body, the blood can be analysed. Blood contains three principle cells, among others: Red blood cells (RBCs), White blood cells (WBCs) and platelets. Out of these only the White cells have a nucleus, and hence the DNA. Occasionally there is a nucleus still within an immature Red cell or platelet. The mother and father should be a 99.9% match. Two closely related individuals will have a higher degree of matching than those not related. DNA matching involves clipping the DNA pieces using Restriction enzymes, preparing them on a nitrocellulose paper and analysing the same electromagnetically. Simple when you know how.'

Cornish had the daunting task of asking the parents for their DNA. They had a prime suspect. Paul Hicks. The landlord at the Star Inn had confirmed that the two men were in the pub on Friday evening and left at 11.30 pm. They now had to prove that Paul Hicks had murdered Finley Jago and that wasn't going to be easy, without a body. But not impossible.

Chapter Twenty-Seven

Maggie Boscawen's funeral procession left St Mawes and made its way to Penmount Crematorium. Steve Boscowan and his son Barry were in one car and Nadine and her children in the other. The vehicles arrived at Kernow Chapel, one of the two chapels on the grounds. Kernow Chapel was slightly smaller and more intimate for a family gathering.

On arrival, the coffin was transferred from the hearse to the panelled-oak wheeled bier which preceded the mourners into the Chapel and was placed within the catafalque. The service was simple with Nadine taking the reading. No one noticed the lonely figure at the back of the Chapel.

At the moment of committal, the curtains were drawn as the coffin was hidden from view until the mourners left the chapel. Maggie's remains were to be placed in a plot alongside her daughter in St Just in Roseland church. Nadine had seen to the arrangements.

Cornish observed what was left of the Pascoe family attending the funeral. For some reason, it brought back memories of her mother's funeral. She was the last of her family alive, except for her daughter who now belonged to someone else's family. All the families she knew were torn apart by something. Where were these so-called perfect families that existed? When something seemed too good to be true the cynic in her rose to the surface. No one escaped the real clutches of life. Even the church admitted the perfect family didn't exist and there were no perfect husbands or ideal wives or in-laws. There were just us sinners. Human beings were flawed, and for that reason, alone Cornish knew she would catch the murderer or killers.

Steve Boscawen was a broken man. Maggie had hidden her darkest secrets from him during their marriage. The day Maggie died they'd had an awful row, and he'd said things in anger which he now regretted. He would live with his actions and consequences for the rest of his life.

Barry sat solemnly beside his father. His mother had been murdered by a coward as far as he was concerned.

Nadine silently wept as her sister's coffin made its final journey. She was devastated and hurt. She and Maggie had always been so close, too close and Maggie had paid the price.

Emma cried for her mother, and not Maggie. Maggie had got in the way of her relationship with Jorey Pomeroy and Emma had taken her revenge. Maggie had fallen head over heels for the wrong person.

Paul felt nothing for Maggie. He never had and never would. He disliked the whole of her family and wanted them all dead and in hell.

Cornish observed the family, more importantly, their prime suspect for Finley Jago's murder. She was just waiting for the DNA results to prove that it was Finley's blood on the ground, enough to assume that he was dead. As Cornish watched the family, she realised that they were all guilty of something. They all had hidden secrets.

There was no one else other than a few friends and local business acquaintances. Maggie Boscawen hadn't been popular.

The reception was held in the Tresanton hotel with its view of the Cornish sea towards St Anthony's lighthouse in the pretty village of St Mawes. It was a feast compared to Lowenna and Roger Pascoe's funerals.

Barry had arranged the catering. It was the least he could do. His father Steve appeared to be in a constant state of inebriation. This wasn't just your simple sandwiches with tea and coffee. No, this was a full spread of Danish pastries, luxury cakes, Cornish cream teas and deep filled sandwiches with fabulous fillings of smoked salmon and cream cheese among others. The cursory sausage rolls were replaced with Melton Mowbray pork pies and English mustard with Rosemary roasted potato wedges and chicken goujons and De Luxe Quiche pieces. The few guests wouldn't forget Maggie Pascoe's funeral in a hurry.

The teas and coffees were abundant alongside the sherry, wine and whiskey for the more hardened drinkers. Most rolled out of the wake at the end.

Jorey Pomeroy sat on the wall above Tavern Beach watching the party. Nobody knew he existed. Maggie's big secret. Maggie was one of his many lovers. He liked to keep it free and easy. A good-looking arty type, women flocked to him for his sexual prowess and laid-back attitude. And not a one-woman man. Jorey couldn't be tamed, many had tried and failed. He was the typical lothario and monogamy was considered a dirty word. It didn't exist in his book. He couldn't get enough of women and when it took his fancy seeing a woman with another woman was positively a turn on. It was somehow loving, sexual and the most natural thing in the world. Jorey had done most things, you name it he'd done it from swinging parties to orgies, and he'd consumed his fair share of what he liked to call recreational drugs. Women were his weakness though when he wasn't consumed by his art, his first love.

Maggie was just like him which had made him want her all the more. She'd had plenty of other men since marrying Steve and could lie and cheat like the best of them. Maggie was an insatiable flirt and loved the attention. She had a fantastic figure, it was her deep green eyes that drew you in. She had driven Jorey mad at times which was why he couldn't let her go, even at the end.

Maggie had many skeletons in her closet, and the biggest one of all had been her confession to Jorey about Barry's father.

Maggie had been dissatisfied early on in her marriage, Steve couldn't get it up and hold it up for long, and it had to be said that he had a poor specimen of manhood. Maggie was bored and lonely which she had declared to Jorey.

'Things are ok between Steve and me. That's the problem, things are just fine but not exciting or even interesting anymore. Our love-making is performed mostly out of habit. If he leaves the dishes in the sink, it makes me furious. Even the way he moves in bed makes me want to stab myself in the eye with a fork.'

That was the last conversation she'd had with Jorey. She knew Steve would never leave her no matter what and wouldn't let her go. They were too entrenched in their past mistakes.

Chapter Twenty-Eight

The butcher's shop was always busy in Truro. Renowned for its homemade pasties and pies and local produce the family-run business had been in existence for over 100 years. They were different to direct from farm meat suppliers as they were professional butchers who farmed. They specialised in suckled native breeds from the area and unique Dexter's and any other old breeds locally. They prided themselves on producing the best quality of meat.

Peter Chegwin had worked there for the last fifty years and knew his trade inside out. He enjoyed his job. People trusted a butcher. What he advised, they heeded. What he recommended they consumed. The apron gave Peter power.

Butchering was propelled by time. The entire early morning was for preparation from sawing the hindquarters of a cow down with a handsaw to cutting the hip on a band saw, then the shank and thumbing out the ribs for short loin. Customers didn't come in to browse, they came in to buy. They wanted answers, and they wanted meat. Peter thought he would get sick of it over time, but there was nothing grim about working in a butcher's shop. When meat had a purpose, a destination, it didn't seem like a wasteful of cultural indulgence. To a butcher, a steak didn't look like a piece of wine-coloured red flesh that was on a cow but a product lovingly prepared and cared for. It looked like someone's dinner. There was no waste, meat got cut for different cuts and economy. Even the fat was used for grease and soap. Bones were sold for soup stock, beef bones packed for dogs. Forty years in the business he had arms like a builder. He enjoyed the knife work, using the heart of the blade. Skill was everything in butchery. One mistake could ruin the cut of meat, worse you could lose a digit. And you couldn't be a butcher if you couldn't deal with people. He'd dealt with people all his life. Butchering and people. That one fatal mistake would now ruin all he had worked for.

He had been living as a Satanist for just over forty years spending most of his life studying theology in his spare time and a small portion as a Jehovah's Witness before becoming disillusioned. When he read the Satanic Bible, it was the first time he had ever felt that he was looking in a mirror. The Satanic Bible was a celebration of life. Do good to those who deserve it and do not waste it on ingrates and, whoever slaps you on your left cheek you smash them on the right. He kept this part of his life separate to his work. Ordinary people wouldn't understand and would struggle to relate to his reasons for Satanism. Peter had joined this local Satanic cult believing he would be with like-minded Satanists. He was a devotee of Anton LaVeyan, author of the Satanic Bible and founder of the Church of Satan. He was wrong. This cult was different, full-blown Devil worshippers, more of the Order of Nine Angels and from what he had witnessed dangerous and deadly.

Peter Chegwin was cleaning up in the shop and disposing of the left-over animal waste. Under the Animal By-

Products Disposal (ABPs) retail butchers had to get rid of their waste in compliance with UK and EU regulations. An authorised carrier collected the ABP and disposed of the animal carcasses and body parts. Peter was responsible for making sure Finlay's body was among the animal debris. He mixed up Finley's already dismembered remains, in the several containers that would be taken away. The receptacles were unlikely to be inspected as the smell would be enough to put any inspector off opening them up.

This would be the last time he would associate with this Satanic cult. He was in too deep to escape their clutches unless he confessed to the police and the disposal of this latest body had invaded his workplace and sanctuary and that wouldn't do. He had felt sickened by his participation in the ritual sacrifices, and Finley's death had intruded a step too far. He could not condone the death of someone so young with a whole life ahead of him. The young girl's demise, although he knew it was wrong had not felt so tragic. He had enjoyed watching her sexually, and he concluded that perhaps her death had represented his hatred for his mother in some strange, macabre way and dislike of women in general. He had never married and had never any time for the opposite sex yet had no homosexual tendencies. He would have made an excellent priest had he chosen that as his vocation.

He would face the music for his part in the young man's death and the others. The police would only have his word about the murders. He had scanned the newspapers and listened to the local news, Finley's death appeared to have gone unnoticed. Perhaps no one seemed to care enough. Peter had already disposed of his remains, so there was no physical proof except at the site possibly where the ritual had taken place. He had no intention of alerting the group to his plans. That would be stupid, and he would be a dead man – for sure.

He was an accessory to murder, three. Finley's was the first body that he had ever dismembered. The only course of action open to him was to contact Cornish. He'd read and listened to her statements given to the press, and he'd rather take his chances with the police than with their Satanic leader.

He had committed the top of the list for Satanic Sins – stupidity. The cardinal sin of Satanism.

Chapter Twenty-Nine

Once again, the Pascoe family were seated in Clemo Nicholl solicitors. Steve Boscawen, Barry Boscawen, Nadine Pascoe and Emma and Paul Hicks. Daggers had been drawn, and neither party would converse with the other. It was an all-out war.

Clemo Nicholl had not looked forward to this meeting. 'Maggie left everything in her will to her only son Barry and according to her wishes a few personal items to the rest of you. The house was part of the family assets so that automatically stays in the estate. Steve, there is a provision for you in Maggie's will that you may remain in the family home. Finally, there is a letter for you Nadine.'

Barry stood up and faced the others.
'I intend to find out which one of you killed my mother. This isn't over.'
He stormed out of the Clemo Nicholl offices.

Nadine hugged Steve and offered her condolences, a mere formality as if he were a stranger. To her, he was no longer part of the family. Like Eddy, her ex-husband he was weak and had no backbone.

He only ever done one thing right in his entire pathetic life and she had witnessed it.

Steve walked into the empty house feeling like an intruder in his own home. He grabbed the bottle taking a swig not caring about anything anymore. He was a dead man. If the booze didn't kill him, then it would only be a matter of time. He considered his options. Keep up the charade for the world to see or fold like a canary, confess and tell all to the police. He didn't want to spend the rest of his years in jail. He looked at his reflection and cried crocodile tears.

Emma walked into her apartment. Maggie had had always been a great aunt until she'd committed her sins against the family. She had to pay for her sins, that was the only way. Traitors had to be dealt with. Satan does not forget. It's not enough to know you have an enemy. Maggie blithely carried out her desires against her and her mother. Emma had loved Maggie and then ripped it away. She had deserved to die.

Nadine read the letter when she got home. If Maggie thought the message would absolve her of any wrongdoing, then she was mistaken and could turn in her grave.

Dear Naddy, I should have told you this a long time ago rather than leave it written down for you to find out if I died before you. I have been unfaithful throughout the whole of my marriage and worst of all I have been unfaithful to you especially given all the pain and suffering we endured together throughout our childhood. You helped me through the loss of my daughter and have always been there for me. I was there for you but not in the way I should have been. I realise that now. I had an affair with your husband Eddy and Barry was the result. I tried to tell you so many times, I just didn't know how to say to you without destroying our relationship. I never meant to hurt you, and I do hope you can find it in your heart to forgive me someday. Love Maggie.

Nadine looked at the letter with bitterness and the contempt it deserved before ripping it up. Maggie hadn't known her real killer.

Chapter Thirty

Cornish and her team were discussing the recent disappearance of Finley Jago. The DNA from the parents proved a match to the blood found at the stones. Gilbert rocked back on his heels, a habit that Cornish had come to expect and one of his many idiosyncrasies.

Gilbert was in his element. He'd been asked to relay his findings and opinion.

'There are lots of ways that you can be fairly confident that people are no longer alive. The body is a central piece of evidence but not critical. The body is helpful if you want to learn how exactly they were killed and if you're going to find evidence from the killer on the body. But sometimes the body isn't as crucial in the investigation such as with cross-contamination. With the evidence and amount of blood at the scene, I would speculate that this young man bled out and died there. Which means his body was then removed and disposed of elsewhere? He wasn't left at the scene to be discovered like Derwa Moon or Sonny. The amount of blood loss is consistent with the last victim

Derwa, and I would surmise that this was another ritual killing given the date. The body was moved to eliminate the evidence of its existence, and those responsible were probably hoping the elements of weather and animals would do the rest. Fortunately for us, the weather held off long enough for us to collect some proof and results. Cornish intervened once Gilbert had finished.

'Let's not forget, the victim's phone suddenly went dead. That's significant. The timing matches and Finley hasn't been seen since, and he's not used his bank account to make any withdrawals, unusual for him, according to his transaction activity on his account. All these things show that Finley Jago isn't with us anymore. We may not have a body but what we do have suggests he's dead. The no body, no murder rule no longer applies. Despite the lack of forensic evidence from the site, I believe that Finley was lured to his death, killed by Paul Hicks and his body taken away to be disposed of, but where? That is the question. It hasn't been found.

Without the body, it will be harder to secure a conviction. Cases of murder where the body has not been found, while uncommon, are not as rare as the public might think. Nationally, there are several each year. So, we need to find a link that can tie this case together. Paul Hicks, I believe is that link, and connects him to both the Satanic killings and the Pascoe murders. We may not get closure for Finley Jago and his parents, but if we could prove Hicks killed the members of his family, then that would be something and a partial result placing him behind bars.

We need to check his phone records against the other murder dates and question Paul Hicks under caution, and we need to persuade Hicks to acknowledge his guilt and tell us where Finley Jago is. This crime was premeditated, and Paul Hicks had the means of concealing Finley's body and a reason to do so.
Let's bring him in for questioning.'

Paul Hicks sat in the interview room in Bodmin headquarters. Clemo Nicholl sat beside him as he was read his rights by Cornish.

'You are under arrest on suspicion of the killing of Finley Jago and disposing of his body. We would also like to question you regarding the recent murders of Roger Pascoe and Maggie Boscawen and the Satanic ritual killing of Sonny the gelding and Derwa Moon, the dates of these murders are in front of you. You do not have to say anything, but it may harm your defence if you do not mention when questioned something which you later rely on in court. Anything you do say may be given in evidence.
You understand your rights?'
'Yes, I understand.'

The mandated audio recording was turned on for the interview. Cornish concentrated on probing the suspect's account of events which she would later compare with the information collated. From the start, it was clear that Paul

Hicks was determined to say nothing. He knew it was his best chance of avoiding prison. That was the last place he was going.

Cornish along with Pearce sat opposite Hicks and his solicitor who looked uncomfortable as Cornish preceded to go through the breakdown of events and the dates. They would systematically be looking for red flags and inconsistencies. The brain was more than capable of creating false memories, human memories were malleable, open to suggestion and often unintentionally false. False memories were everywhere, in everyday situations where people failed to notice their mistake or care. Everyone made errors or misremembered things with grave consequences for the criminal justice system.

The questioning had been going on for hours, several coffee breaks had been taken, and their suspect was steadfast in his refusal to talk. Eventually, tiredness appeared to get the better of Paul Hicks, and his tune changed.

'Where were you on the night that Roger Pascoe and Derwa Moon were killed?'

'I was at home, in bed, asleep alone. Why would I kill my grandfather?'

'You tell us? Was it because of the abuse?'

'I told you about the abuse in the first place so why would I tell you if that was the possible reason for killing him, which I've already told you I didn't do?'

Cornish drummed her fingers on the table impatiently.

'Are you a practising Satanist Paul?'

'No.'

'Maggie Boscawen was murdered on Friday 15 March in the morning. Where were you?'

'I was at one of the many properties that we rent out sorting out a water leak along with the plumber. You can check out my alibi.'

Clemo Nicholl conveniently handed DS Pearce a sheet of paper with the plumber's details and the address of the property where they met up.

'What about Finley Jago. You picked him up on Godrevy Beach and took him down to St Just Penwith and the Star Inn, correct?'

'There's no law about meeting people and taking them out for a good time. He was going to kill himself earlier that day, and I decided to cheer him up. That's not against the law is it the last time I checked?'

'Murder is though. After the pub, you took Finley to Kenidjack Common where you killed him. His blood was found there.'

A muscle twitched in Paul Hicks jaw as Cornish rattled his cage. And Paul Hicks eyes darted to the left while he fabricated the next part of his story.

'No. I left him at the pub and drove away. He wanted to stay down there, and I drove home. I wasn't his keeper. That's all I know. I've nothing further to say.'

'Take him away. DS Pearce, please escort Mr Hicks into custody. You're not going anywhere for the moment Mr Hicks.'

Cornish stood up and looked directly at Paul Hicks. Hicks was scum, posh scum and the dreg of society and his money wouldn't protect him from the law. And Cornish could see it in his eyes. He was guilty. She just had to prove it, and for the moment Cornish had nothing. Paul Hicks had implied that Finley had mentioned he was in trouble at home and when they left the Star Inn he was alive, and he didn't see him afterwards. Cornish didn't believe him, and the law was on her side for the moment. They would hold Paul Hicks for the maximum time allowed, the full ninety-six hours if necessary. Murder was a serious crime, and Cornish could feel herself beginning to lose patience.

Cornish wanted answers and fast.

'What's the status on Paul Hicks mobile phone records from the provider?'

Pearce had the latest information.

'According to his phone on the night of the first killing, the gelding, Sonny, Paul Hicks phone was still in Padstow. Again, the same for the night of Roger Pascoe and Derwa Moon. We can't place him near the crime scenes. The same for Maggie Boscawen. He was definitely with the plumber at the address given, that all checks out. We can place him with Finley at the Star Inn but nothing afterwards. His phone was on in the area until 12.30, after that, the signal moves as he drives home.'

'That doesn't mean Paul Hicks didn't commit these murders. It just makes him very clever. He probably deliberately left his mobile phone at home. From what you say it would appear that Finley Jago wasn't exactly planned. An opportunity presented itself at the right time.

Does Hicks have a second mobile that we don't know about and is untraceable?'

'Not that we've found' Ma'am.

'What about his DNA?' asked Cornish.

'We're waiting on the results. We might get lucky and get a match for the DNA found on Derwa's body.'

'Let's see whether being in a cell for the night changes his mind' replied Cornish.

'Maggie Boscawen is the odd one out at the moment. Her murder appears to be a crime of passion, not the act of a sadistic cold-blooded killer. Let's look at the husband and what about a lover somewhere in the shadows.

This is one slippery fish, and our priority so let's get to it and catch the bastard.

I was born here and have spent my life getting to know this land. I'll turn over every pebble on the beach and every grain of sand if I have to.'

Chapter Thirty-One

Peter Chegwin wanted to put this all behind him and move on with his life.

'Take one day at a time, one step at a time.'

He walked into Bodmin police headquarters and asked to speak to the person in charge, DCI Cornish. Now he was seated in a windowless room with just a table and three extra chairs, and no smoking, that didn't bother him. He'd never smoked in his entire life. He declined a solicitor. He was ready to take any punishment coming his way. In his eyes, he would be safer inside a prison cell than outside.

Cornish and Pearce sat opposite this diminutive man with broad shoulders, arms like a bodybuilder and large hands capable of hauling and chopping up carcasses. He had all the skillset necessary for murder. Cornish recited the usual caution.

Chegwin explained his interest in the occult and how he'd found and joined this Satanic Cult that the papers were going on about.

'I've been through hell because of this, living with the horror of what I've done since that day. Every minute of every day has been a nightmare since I joined this group. This is not the way of a true Satanist, a follower of Anton LaVeyan, author of the Satanic Bible and founder of the Church of Satan.

The leader of the group, the Grand Master, is cold and calculating and dangerous from what I have seen. This cult is different, full-blown Devil worshippers, more of the Order of Nine Angels (ONA), dangerous and deadly. They take things a step too far performing evil acts for its own sake. They believe in Satan as a real entity and support violence, murder, hatred and evil.

I've regretted my participation in the rituals, but I couldn't extricate myself. I can't take any more of the pain. Our leader made it abundantly clear what would happen to me. I know the wrong can't be changed, but this is the closest I can come to doing the right thing. I can't live any longer with the guilt and want to clear my conscience.'

'Do you know the names of the others in the group?' Cornish enquired.

'No, I don't know who they are.'
That wasn't strictly true. And if he could find out so easily, it wouldn't take the police long, and Peter was sure they must have some idea. He was only prepared to go so far.
'I was contacted by phone and given instructions on where to meet. We donned our robes on arrival, and I only saw their faces lit up by torchlight. I've never met them during the day. It wasn't necessary to have such personal contact, and the leader didn't encourage that. They use the Seven-Fold Way – aka Seven-Fold Sinister Way for their system of training used by traditional Order of Nine Angels nexions, the guided practice of the Dark Arts. The Way is an individual one: each stage, of the seven stages that make the Way, is achieved by the individual as a result of their own effort. You work mostly on your own and come

together for the rituals and gatherings. I was an Initiate along with another man in the group. The two women were much higher than me, they were referred to as Mistress of Earth.'

'What did you do with Finley Jago's body?'
'I disposed of it with the left-over animal waste. Under the Animal By-Products Disposal (ABPs) retail butchers have to get rid of their waste using an authorised carrier to dispose of the animal carcasses and body parts. Finlay's body was cut up at the ritual site on Kenidjack Common. And I disposed of it; I mixed it in among the animal debris. The containers have already been taken away. You'll never find his body parts.

I would like to add that my part in the rituals was motivated by my belief that I had found a like-minded group. I now realise how wrong I was. I now wish to avoid the pain, further disappointment and hurt to these families that have suffered by my admission. No one else outside the group knows anything about my part in this or my disposal of the body of the young man. Had anyone known they would have reported me to the police. Apart from this statement, I will exercise my right to silence.'

Peter Chegwin eased back in his chair relieved that he had got his confession off his chest. He felt the pressure and burden had been somehow lifted. He wasn't a cold-blooded killer, far from it. But he had played his part, and for that, he would take his punishment.

'The other Initiate delivered the young woman to the Grand Master, that's all I know. Do you have any suspects?'

'We do have someone we suspect. Would you look at some photographs for us?'

Pearce produced some photos and laid them out in front of Peter Chegwin who had no hesitation in pointing to a picture of Paul Hicks.

Cornish knew that few murderers actually confessed. In fact, they would go to great lengths to avoid being implicated as they knew the consequences would be severe. They were going to have to investigate the matter thoroughly and get the evidence to back up Chegwin's statement. They hadn't got any forensic evidence to link Paul Hicks to the scenes. Cornish had identified Hicks as the most likely suspect for the murders, Chegwin had confirmed this, but without something concrete, they could only hold Hicks for long.

Hicks, arrested, had been sitting in his cell. They had passed the first 24 hours, and no charges had been brought. A further 12-hour extension, authorised by Jane Falconbridge, had come and gone and the latest application made to the magistrate's court in Truro for an additional 36-hour extension was nearing its completion. Meanwhile, Hicks had been fed and watered and given designated rest and sleep periods complements of Devon and Cornwall Police. Several interviews had revealed nothing more. Hicks had been given his opportunity to give his side of the story, provide any alibis or defence to the allegations. He was one cool customer. Clemo Nicholl had appeared more concerned than Hicks who maintained his right to silence. They still had nothing conclusive, and the custody clock was running out of time. Even with Peter Chegwin's version of events, there was no evidence to charge Hicks, and it looked as if he would be given police bail to return to the police station at a specific time and date by which time Cornish hoped their investigation would be complete. 'Your statement will be taken into account, and I do suggest you get yourself a lawyer Mr Chegwin. Will you voluntarily allow us to take your DNA?'

'Yes, am I to be arrested?'

'Mr Chegwin, whether you are charged or requisitioned, you will need to sign the sheet setting out the offences for which you could be charged and your voluntary statement today. These serious offences can be tried in the Magistrates Court or Crown Court, and there are no time limits to the trial time. The police will have to conduct their investigation into your statement and allegations before any charges can be brought. We will be in touch with you, I strongly urge you to get legal representation. And, don't leave the county without contacting us first.'

Peter Chegwin walked out of the Police Station a dejected man. He didn't have a clue what the future held for him. His name would be plastered in the papers and associated with these murders forever.

In the Order of Nine Angels Black Book of Satan he had now committed the Satanic Sin – Die rather than submit. There was only one option open to Chegwin – death. By his own hand or by another and he didn't need any guess as to who that would be. It would be only a matter of time.

Chapter Thirty-Two

Cornish had her team working round the clock. They needed a breakthrough, and that came in the form of Elizabeth Baker from the London School of Economics and Political Science (LSE). An eminent Professor of Sociology with Special Reference to the Study of Religion. Her primary interest was cult sects and new religious movements. Baker was prolific on the lecture scene around the world and a familiar commentator on religious issues on radio and television. With countless publications under her name Baker was the guru to ask.

'The so-called Satanist ONA is fake and has been all along. Successful marketing hype, nothing more. A phantom organisation that someone has created. This is merely a hardcore Satanist group led by this person calling himself the Grand Master and putting a different spin on his beliefs. They are not a functioning Occult order let alone a Satanist one. The group is small, non-political from what I can see on the website and looking to attract people who have the potential to be useful to their cause. From what you say the leader is capable of persuasion. Most cults used women followers to Honeytrap other male followers. Other groups claiming to be ONA have tendencies towards neo-Nazi behaviour, but this group in Cornwall doesn't appear to have any connection to those groups. I would suggest that this group is a splinter faction of Anton LaVeyan and is adopting a set of beliefs to suit their own purpose.

Neither is the leader a serial killer. That's not an accurate description of his crimes. When serial killers murder, they tend to have an emotional cooling-off period between murders. This is an important factor. They slip back into normal lives in between deaths to appear completely normal functioning human beings until the urge to kill becomes overwhelming, and they strike again. What you seem to have is consistent with a killing spree with no emotional cooling-off period between the incidents. The killing spree is cold-blooded, calculated and planned. Also, you have 'mission killers', a Satanic Cult carrying out Ritual sacrifices for a belief.

Over the years I've discovered that there is crime pure and simple (gangland, gun-crazed killers) and terrorist crime (political) to a religious deviation and usually evil, messianic, sadistic of a 'death cult'. We treat ordinary crime – killing of Westerners by Westerners for money, greed, personal revenge or drug-related as normal. Terrorist crimes almost always indicate Muslims are responsible. In other words, criminals are ours while terrorists are dark-skinned Muslims who hate our values. These killings from what you describe are linked but only by the thread that the same killer is murdering with a purpose for money and power possibly and that their Satanic beliefs are encouraging them and giving them the feeling of a higher ambition and self-belief in them achieving their end game. For whatever reason your killer has escalated quickly, something set off these killings. You, Detective Chief Inspector need to find out what that is.'

Cornish suspected that good old-fashioned greed was the reason. She still needed a confession or proof that placed Hicks precisely in the frame. The team were exhausted, and Hicks had been released without charge.

Cornish watched Hicks walk out of the Police Headquarters and face the media. He smiled for the cameras.

'I have been labelled an evil killer, a Satanist and linked to the deaths in my family. You, my friends, know this isn't the case. I have never been an angel, but I am not what some sections of the media are portraying. I am convinced the truth will prevail. It may take months, years. However long it takes it doesn't matter. It will eventually emerge.

Outside a storm was brewing and Cornish hoped it wasn't an omen for worse to come.

Chapter Thirty-Three

Jorey Pomeroy had never known loss like losing Maggie. What they had shared had been real to both of them even if they wouldn't admit it. He'd watched her funeral from the back of the chapel and cried silently as her body was carried past him to her final resting place.

Jorey knew that when you lost someone, you didn't just lose them when you said goodbye. You didn't even lose them when you said your final I love you or watched them when they left your studio apartment for the last time. You didn't just lose them once, you lost them every single day since the day they left you. Maggie was still everywhere in his space, in his bed, her favourite coffee mug was in his kitchen that he now used all the time and, in his head, when he played his music. He should have told her how he really felt then maybe, just maybe, she would still be alive today.

He should have fought harder for her, convinced her to stay. There was no going back. Their love would never be forgotten. They had shared their secrets, their hearts and he was her forever person, his come-hell-or-high-water. Maggie knew his faults. But here was the thing about life: It worked in funny and sometimes unfortunate ways. The people who could have been there forever were sometimes the very ones you had to let go – often for reasons that were entirely outside of your control.

How did you say goodbye to that person you thought would be by your side for the rest of your life? How do you let forever go? If Jorey had committed this crime, even if he had, it would have been because he loved her too much, right?

The handwriting had been on the wall, for the people around, for the family, for the friends, more importantly for Maggie who had ignored and believed that maybe it wasn't what she thought.

Jorey was overcome with grief. Inconsolable. Murders can occur in clusters, be contagious. Jorey's death would be added to that toll. In the last few days, Jorey had the realisation that every breath was more painful than the last. He was in the darkest place he had ever been and could see no way out. The pain had to stop. He'd been through painful moments before, but nothing compared to now. Alone in his kitchen that morning the plan had quickly begun to take shape. He knew what would be effective, hopefully, the quickest and least painful. He swallowed the tablets and lay down on the bed. Death would come to him soon enough as he closed his eyes.

Lying on the bed, Jorey kept his eyes closed and waited to die. He kept thinking about his dog that he would miss so much and trying to relax to let the sleep take him away from all this pain. Except it didn't work out like that. He felt the dizziness kick in and went through periods of profuse sweating all over his body. His whole body became itchy, and his breathing laboured. His heart pounded uncontrollably, and after a while, he glanced at his clock to see what the time was, and the blurred light danced up and down. The slightest movement resulted in his world swirling around like swinging a cloth underwater. He couldn't raise his head off the pillow let alone sit up. He closed his eyes again and laid there waiting for it to pass, this hell, that was only the beginning. Jorey felt really fucked up, and as soon as the realisation hit him, he no longer wanted to die anymore. He had lain for hours feeling like shit, wanting to vomit and wanting to live until finally, he felt his body easing out of the immense discomfort allowing him to feel a sense of having come through the worse and he would live to tell the tale. He made a mental note to himself never to repeat this unpleasant experience and nightmare. He would never have the guts to try again. He finally fell asleep.

The rope had been thrown over the beam in Jorey's workshop. Jorey stood on the chair, swaying slightly as the loop was placed over his head around his neck. The chair was pushed away. His neck didn't break. Instead, he hung there slowly drifting off towards unconsciousness. There was no pain, just peace, his body didn't fight. He had accepted his fate as he drifted off to meet his maker.

Pearce grabbed Jorey Pomeroy's legs and held him as Mac loosened the rope.
'Bloody lucky we were here. A few more minutes and you would have been dead.'

Jorey didn't know where he was at first. The last thing he remembered was lying down on his bed. Now he was semi-conscious and throwing up in a bucket.

'The ambulance is on its way. Just lie down on your side.'
Mac placed him in the recovery position and covered him with a blanket that happened to be lying around.
Pearce interrupted.
'So, you were trying to hang yourself?'
Jorey was compos mentis enough to know that hadn't been his plan.
'I just took some pills and wanted to go to sleep, that was all. How did I get here?'

Pearce looked around Jorey's studio apartment and found the pills by his daybed.

'Let's get you to the hospital, examined and then I'll take down your version of events.'

Pearce and Mac looked around Jorey's studio. Nothing had been taken although Jorey's space was cluttered. Clutter caused confusion to most people, but Pearce suspected most artists were handicapped when it came down to organisation. Creative people were visual and retrieved memory from visual clues, hence the reason why an artist would have piles of stuff lying around to see everything they were working on or for inspiration. The room was full of materials, hand-made objects, photographs and living and organic things. Bingo.

It was the photographs that caught Pearce and Mac's attention. A provocative pose of a naked woman on Jorey's bed, no mistaking Maggie Boscawen and Emma Hicks in the photographs. Clearly and from looking at the pictures, they seemed comfortable with the intimate act that Jorey had committed to film. Clearly, Jorey liked keeping his special memories around him.

The doctor on duty at Truro hospital informed Pearce and Mac that the number of tablets Jorey claimed to have taken and produced his symptoms would have only given him a thorough night's sleep. He needed to have taken double the amount to have caused severe harm, possibly death. Jorey didn't have a clue, he couldn't remember a thing and swore blind it had never occurred to him to hang himself.

Cornish had to admit.

'Accidental strangulation is rare but does happen, usually when a tie or scarf or the such like gets caught in something. Hanging a man by pushing him off a chair and making it look like a suicide? The police will have a tough time proving it wasn't suicide. How can we prove a hanging suicide was actually a staged murder? We need means and motive and evidence to prove the crime. With the discovery of the photographs, we may have a clue into Maggie's private life.'

Pearce had discovered further information by speaking to a few people. He knew the locals in St Mawes and had managed to find out through the grapevine that Maggie and Jorey were having an affair. Fortunately for Jorey, he was alive to tell the tale. Usually, the only person that can answer the question of why they wanted to take their own life was dead.

'I was inconsolable after Maggie's death. I just wanted to be at peace.'

'We found photographs in your studio of Maggie Boscawen and Emma Hicks.'

'Emma and I had a relationship some time ago. You are probably aware she, Emma, swings both ways. Anyway, after that Maggie and I got together, and Emma was angry, furious. I'd see Maggie several times a week, either at my place or the studio. Sometimes we played outdoors. Steve didn't know.'

Cornish interrupted.

'Maggie was very wealthy, you knew that? Did you kill her? You can see how this looks for you, can't you?'

'No, why would I do that when I loved her. I knew she wouldn't leave Steve. She'd told me that. Why I don't know because he was an asshole. All I know is that Barry isn't Steve's son. Eddy Hicks is Barry's father.'

Chapter Thirty-Four

Steve Boscawen hadn't slept in days since Maggie's funeral. Was there such a thing as loving someone too much? He had smothered Maggie and had consequently pushed her away many times. She had made him display signs of insecurity and selfishness trying to hold on to her when she crossed the line. She was like a bird wanting to fly away, and he had continually tried to clip her wings and failed. She would often disappear for days at a time but would always turn up apologetic. Their marriage had been one long rollercoaster of highs and lows and Maggie's affairs.

Steve knew about Maggie and Jorey Pomeroy from the very start. And he knew about Jorey's abilities in the bedroom. It was common knowledge that he was hung like a donkey and had the stamina of a stallion. Steve paled into insignificance compared to the likes of the Jorey's of this world, and it pissed him off. Maggie had threatened to leave Steve in the past and hadn't. Her recent warnings he'd taken seriously. Something had changed. And he was concerned that he wouldn't be able to keep her his for much longer. Maggie had been acting differently, and he assumed it was because of Jorey.

Steve's drinking escalated when Maggie had affairs. He wouldn't usually describe himself as a drunk. He would have a few drinks but never get to the complete drunkenness state. He could drive, work, speak in public, and no one would notice. Feeling neither happy or sad, just detached from himself. It was the only way he could handle Maggie's affairs. He'd been teetotaller on several occasions, but Maggie's behaviour always made him reach for the bottle. He hated himself for being so weak and lapsing back. Sobriety was his punishment. He lost weight, felt physically better, slept better. And still, Maggie still didn't fancy him or curtail her affairs. Drinking took away that pain of realisation.

In the end, Steve only wanted to love her more than anyone else. More than the stars in the sky, more than the blood in his veins. And so, selfishly, this last time when Maggie pulled away from him, the last argument when she slammed the door to take Frank for his walk, he was scared that he had lost her for good and wanted to make everything right. And so, he did the only thing he could think to do.

Chapter Thirty-Five

The leader of the Satanic Cult had failed to carry out his plan. Jorey was still alive.

Jorey had joined their group, knew their most intimate secrets and had threatened to reveal them. Traitors needed to be punished. The only reason Jorey was still alive was that he didn't know who had tried to kill him and failed. The police had no evidence and no leads.

He knew all their dirty little secrets. Barry had no clue that Steve wasn't his father, Steve considered Barry was his son, and neither had any inkling that Jorey knew, or so he thought.

Jorey would naturally assume Steve was the obvious choice for trying to kill him. He must have found out about his affair with Maggie.

He would be on the completely wrong track.

Jorey was done. Done with the lying, the secrecy, and now Maggie was dead; he needed to see Steve face to face. He'd been having his cake and eating it for far too long, devouring another man's wife. He couldn't move on until he'd put this behind him. It was eating away at him.
Steve, dishevelled, opened the front door. He knew Jorey by sight having spied on the lovers.
'I suppose you want to come in and gloat then?'

Jorey walked into Maggie's house for the first time. Maggie had always come to his place. The opulence struck him. But, behind the façade of wealth, there was a feeling of emptiness. The house was furnished beautifully, yet devoid of any character and warmth as if the occupants just lived there but didn't belong. It was missing that 'je ne se quoi'.

Jorey looked at the man sitting opposite him. He was a mess. It was apparent he had been drinking and hadn't shaved in days. This man looked defeated, dejected, and that made Jorey feel worse. He'd come here hoping to absolve himself and feel better about Maggie's death, but he had no place being here. Surviving infidelity was not easy. And surviving it when the other person had died was even worse. Steve was a broken man.

Steve looked up and spoke.
'Maggie was a pathological liar and a serial adulterer. She couldn't stop. If it hadn't been you, then it would have been someone else.'
As Steve recited the carefully rehearsed words, he knew they were a lie. This affair had been different. Steve had sensed that from the beginning. And Maggie was going to leave him. She had said as much just not in so many words. It was her actions that had made it clear that day. And he couldn't have that.

Looking across at Jorey Steve felt sorry for the man and at the same time pleased. Jorey was suffering, he had truly loved Maggie, and that had surprised Jorey to realise the depth of his feelings and love for her. Jorey was genuinely in pain and suffering. The punishment for the rest of his life would be that Jorey knew he was responsible for what happened to Maggie. He may not have strangled Maggie, but he had inadvertently caused her death.

Jorey didn't get the answers he had come looking for. He didn't get an admission from Steve that he had murdered his wife. He left feeling worse than before wishing he had died. His life had been spared so that he could feel the pain and the loss for the rest of his life.

Steve closed the door and looked at himself in the mirror. He looked like shit. He smiled.
'Fuck you Maggie and fuck you, Jorey Pomeroy.'

Chapter Thirty-Six

Cornish was having a bad day. The media frenzy was saying that there was a serial killer in Cornwall and the Pascoe family had been targeted. Cornish had already contacted a well-known professor of sociology and criminology and had found out some intriguing information which she was explaining to her team.

'We have had a spate of murders in Cornwall. Three in one family so far if we count Lowenna Pascoe's drowning and two further murders, the horse Sonny and Derwa Moon both under the guise of a satanic ritual and now Finley Jago. Someone also tried to kill Jorey Pomeroy and failed. Whoever murdered the others made sure they died. They wouldn't have made this type of mistake in letting their victim live. Maybe they were interrupted. It was lucky for Jorey that Pearce and Mac turned up.

Serial killers are motivated according to Professor Baker in many ways. Material gain is a primary motive for most, known as comfort/gain killers. This type of killer selects their own targets and commits murder in response to an emotional need for comfort or security. Their victims are often family members, close acquaintances but after they've killed, they usually wait for a while to allow any suspicion to subside. Jorey doesn't fit with this profile. This killer was in a hurry so what was their motive?'

Mac wanted to impress Cornish.

'Ma'am, the age-old motive has to be money.'

Pearce interrupted.

'Good old-fashioned revenge?'

Hutchens raised an interesting point.

'Jorey knew too much? The time frame's also important. There are three family members left who inherit a substantial fortune and within a time frame. The countdown is already on. Should they die during the estate administration, then the remaining grandchildren receive in equal parts, outside that, it would form part of that person's own estate.'

Cornish continued.

'We're missing something. Let's go back over all the statements and double check the alibis. I want Jorey Pomeroy questioned again, in the interview room if we have to. And a DNA sample taken.'

Jorey Pomeroy sat opposite Cornish and Hutchens while Cornish read Jorey his rights. He declined legal representation. Sitting opposite the two women, Jorey sat with one leg crossed indolently over the over. The mark where the rope had dug into his neck ached, and he rubbed it. Cornish and Hutchens followed the direction of Jory's myopic gaze as he watched a spider abseil to the ceiling.

Cornish commenced the line of questioning.
'Jorey, Maggie Boscawen did not die as Mother Nature intended.'

'I don't know what you want from me?'
'Why don't you chat about how you met Maggie?'
'That's easy, through Emma.'

Cornish was interested in where this was leading.

'Go on.'

'Emma and I had been going out for some time. When I say going out, we were more like fuck buddies really. I was the flavour of that month if you like. Emma swings both ways, and we occasionally had a ménage à trois. Emma introduced me to Maggie one day and I started seeing Maggie. She was gagging for it if you know what I mean. Emma and I went our separate ways. Maggie would pop round to my apartment or the studio where I worked, and we just fucked.'

Jorey didn't want to admit to Cornish that it was any more than a casual affair. The less said, the better.

'Was Maggie seeing anyone else?'

'I wouldn't know. I wasn't her keeper. Like I said we just fucked.'

Hutchens handed Jorey a paper with dates on.

'What were you doing on these dates?'

'How the hell do I know?'

'I suggest you take a good look and answer the question.' Cornish was in no mood for games.

Jorey looked at the sheet in front of him and shuffled uneasily in his chair. He needed to regain his composure and quickly.

Emma had warned Jorey about the best techniques to resist interrogation. She knew that police interviews weren't designed to break someone, and interview rooms were not as miserable as portrayed on the television. They couldn't coerce a confession out of him, that was worse than no confession at all because silence could be interpreted whereas coercion must be reacted to. Emma told him to say nothing, remain silent. If he wanted zero exchange of information, and to be recompensed, then he had to stay tight-lipped.

Cornish was hoping Jorey might want to get over his side of the story. He didn't look like a killer, a lover yes, a killer, no. Very rarely did anyone choose to remain silent when given the opportunity to explain.

'What's this all about? I've done nothing wrong. If you're accusing me of something, then I want a lawyer.'

Cornish wanted answers.

'These dates Jorey. Where were you?'

'Sunday 7 January I would have been in bed, alone. Friday 19 January I would have been in the Victory Inn in St Mawes, my local. Friday 2 February I would have been in the pub again, and I was in my studio working the day Maggie was killed. Can I go now? Unless you want to charge me with something.'

Hutchens and Cornish let him talk looking sympathetic. Jorey didn't know it, but he was trying to smooth over his involvement with Maggie to make himself look better and explain away any evidence the police might have. By letting Joey talk, Cornish hoped that he would tie his own noose.

Hutchens had written everything Jorey said down. He wouldn't beat interviewing detectives on their home turf.

Cornish and Hutchens watched Jorey exit the police station. This was going to be a tough case to crack.

'Hutchens check out those dates. Pearce and Mac check all the statements again. We have another lead. Jorey and Emma Hicks were an item at one time.'

Jorey Pomeroy was pleased with himself. He had said as little as possible. He shouldn't have said anything at all, but that wasn't his way. It might have been Emma's, after all, she was a rigid, uptight bitch. A good fuck but she not only fucked you physically she fucked your mind. The last time they spoke had been over Maggie. They'd had a lovers' fight and called it a day. The trickiest thing about a lovers' tiff is that it's hard to remember who first hurt who but in this case that was easy. For the first time in his life, Jorey Pomeroy had been upstaged by a woman.

Chapter Thirty-Seven

Cornish had her own view on the murders which she was updating to Jane Falconbridge.

'Practically everyone wants to murder someone. There is no such thing as the perfect murder. How many times do we see the murderer eating at the end of a movie having got away with it? No, the murderer always gets caught. There may be twists and turns to solve but, in the end, we get our man or woman. Or not if there's insufficient evidence. But I would want that person to know that I know they did it. And I would figure out some way to prove it eventually. They would always be looking over their shoulder because I'd be there in the background somewhere observing. So, I don't think about the perfect murder, the one that went to plan and without a hitch. When there is murder, there are always hitches. I think about the outcome: Cheese, villa, laughing, counting their money and then they get caught. The world is right again.'

Falconbridge didn't doubt for one minute that Cornish wouldn't solve the cases. She was dogmatic and thorough and more determined than any other police officer she had ever met. A keen observer of people and their foibles. They'd had a few tough cases in the past, and not many perpetrators had slipped through the net. Modern policing techniques had improved the chances of getting caught. The police were gaining ground every day as technology developed.

Pearce was the first to find a loophole in Jorey Pomeroy's statement.

'Friday 2 February Jorey wasn't in his usual, the Victory Inn St Mawes. In fact, the landlord noticed because he's always there on Friday and Saturday evenings. Never misses.'

'So where was he that night?'

Cornish wanted to know what Jorey Pomeroy was up to. He was hiding something, she was sure of that.

'There's more' continued Pearce. 'There was another rumour circulating around St Mawes that Maggie Boscawen was planning on leaving her husband according to her hairdresser.'

Hairdressers were the fountain of knowledge for gossip and a catch up while getting their hair done. They often knew more about their clients love lives and medical problems than even their family and friends.

Hutchens and Mac had been going over Paul Hicks statement.
'We decided to go back to the Fishermans Arms in St Merryn to speak to the manager. Paul Hicks wasn't in on Friday 2 February. He definitely wasn't a regular. No one remembers who Derwa went off with. What the manager did say though was the bloke didn't live locally, he would have recognised him else. And he was definitely Cornish judging by the accent and arty looking. You know the types with their harem pants, that was how he described him.'

Cornish wondered.

'Sounds more like the Jorey Pomeroy's of this world.'

Any chance we can get a picture of Jorey Pomeroy over there. My gut says he's involved somehow.'

'We can pull off an image from the police CCTV camera' replied Mac.

'Get over there straight away' said Cornish with a matter of urgency. 'Someone has already tried to kill Jorey Pomeroy once. I don't want them to succeed on the second attempt.'

The manager in the Fishermans Arms was most helpful. The last thing he wanted was the pub to be involved given the owner's celebrity status. He recognised Jorey Pomeroy straight away from the photograph.

DS Pearce called Cornish straight away. This could be a matter of life or death for Jorey Pomeroy.

Chapter Thirty-Eight

Jorey Pomeroy was in his workshop creating his latest masterpiece when his visitor arrived. He'd been contemplating going back to the police and confessing, but he knew he would be dead for sure if he did that. He didn't have any option other than to keep his mouth firmly shut – forever. And, live with what he had done. He'd made the mistake of trying to exit himself from the group and once in you could never escape.

'What do you want. I told you I'm done.'

'Well, you can't just call it a day. I'll decide when it's over, not you.'

'I don't care what you fucking do to me. I'm not playing any more of your games. I didn't sign up for this.'

'Calm down Jorey. Let's have a drink and discuss this sensibly.'

'I see you've come prepared then' as the caller unscrewed the bottle of wine and poured two glasses. What Jorey failed to notice was the addition of the tasteless liquid, Phenobarbital, in a dosage that would kill him.

Jorey sipped his red wine and began to relax. He was talking and reminiscing about old times. They had always been at ease with each other, and it was such a shame that it was going to end this way for Jorey.

The symptoms quickly took hold, his vision blurred, and he felt himself slowly getting tired. All he wanted to do was put his head down. He watched his guest place the extra wine glass away, and he knew they would never be friends again.

Jorey had fulfilled his part of the deal in assisting in the delivery and death of the young woman Derwa. He hadn't realised what would happen to her. He had thought it was just a bit of fun. He knew now he would never be able to escape their clutches. This was probably the best way out. He had hated himself for being part of their stupid cult.

Taking part in Derwa's sacrifice, assisting in her rape and mutilation had left him physically sick. Finley Jago's death hadn't affected him as much. The man was a bottom feeder and would never amount to anything. The horse Sonny had upset him the most. He loved animals. They gave unconditional love.

As he lay down on his daybed, he finally felt at peace. Maggie had gone, and he realised all too late why Maggie had died and who had killed her. Revenge was a funny thing and getting someone else to kill Maggie had been very clever.

The best revenge as a spurned lover really was to fuck the best friend and then kill them both.

Chapter Thirty-Nine

Cornish and Hutchens were the first to arrive at Jorey Pomeroy's art studio. The door was unlocked, and they walked in to find him lying on a daybed. Cornish felt his pulse and realised they were too late.

The coroner's van would be required, and Emma Bray was the unfortunate CO on duty, once again.

Cornish and Hutchens scanned the workshop. It was a typical artists abode, full of clutter and mayhem. The only thing noticeable was the bottle of red wine on the table and one glass. From the outward signs, one could be forgiven for jumping to the conclusion that Jorey had attempted suicide for the alleged second time in so many days. Cornish didn't buy that idea. Someone, who, they didn't know, had failed the first time around and had now made sure that Jorey would die this time. He wouldn't get a second reprieve.

The CO van arrived at the same time as Emma Bray along with Turner and having declared Jorey Pomeroy dead his limbs were sealed, and he was labelled for delivery to Gilbert back at base camp.

The workshop was designated a crime scene area, and a careful as possible walkthrough, and appraisal of the scene was carried out by Turner. This case was proving to be the most challenging for the force for some time. Cornish wanted answers and a result quickly.

Falconbridge now wanted daily updates on the progress.; the body count was rising. Cornish had hoped to ascertain the motive from Jorey Pomeroy. That was never going to happen now. He had been a loose end. It would be back to the board.

They were missing something vitally important in cracking this case.

Chapter Forty

Jorey Pomeroy's tattooed body would have been a nightmare to catalogue for the police years ago. Now they were allowed to take photographs of the body for reference which was lucky in Jorey's case.

Gilbert didn't know whether to read them. Every tattoo had a story, probably in Jorey's case of irresponsibility, friendship, a trip abroad or memory to keep. Some were artistic and beautiful, others appeared to have been rushed, amateurish, even self-made.

Tattoos told us something about a person, whether that person intended them to or not. And Gilbert knew they weren't cheap. Jorey Pomeroy didn't look like a person who regretted his tattoos, but there were plenty of people who did.

Tattoo removal clinics were on the rise, and most tattoo parlours offered tattoo removal now. Gilbert knew the average tattoo took twelve sessions to remove at a substantial cost and up to two years. What the tattooists didn't say, and Gilbert knew, was that in case studies of skin cancer malignant skin cells were found to have been re-seeded by the tattoo needle. In other words, the low-grade inflammation caused by tattoo inks could raise a person's risk of skin cancers.

Gilbert set about dissecting Jorey's body. This young man had died in the prime of his life with no children, that he knew of, and no legacy for the next generation. A talented artist by all accounts Gilbert had been informed.

There appeared to be no stray strands of DNA on the body, and the only sign of poisoning would be on the tests on the blood and stomach contents. The results were conclusive. Jorey Pomeroy had been poisoned using Phenobarbital, a barbiturate drug that doctors usually prescribe for its sedative and anti-seizure properties. If a doctor had prescribed the medication, then Jorey would have been advised not to drink alcohol which would significantly increase the barbiturate's sedative and depressant effects on the brain. There appeared to be nothing in the GP report to indicate Jorey was on any medication other than self-prescribed.

Cornish was listening to Gilbert's findings.
'Phenobarbital acts on the central nervous system and its effect with alcohol would have depended on the amounts of each taken. It would have worked within ten minutes to an hour after ingestion again depending on the amount of food Jorey had in his stomach. Drowsiness would have followed, and his breathing would have slowed down. A large enough dose was administered to depress his heartbeat, reduce blood pressure and cause his circulation to fail which resulted in his death.
From examining the deceased and the evidence, the wine glass, it would suggest that the Phenobarbital was administered as a liquid into his red wine.

The drug is metabolised by the liver and excreted in the urine, but it can be easily detected for up to fifteen days after a dose. The addition of alcohol increased side effects. Jorey was merely put to sleep, permanently.

Someone intended to kill Jorey Pomeroy? The dose was too high for anyone to administer themselves unless they wanted to commit suicide and from what you say he preferred tablets as the quick and painless way out. I doubt if he even knew about this type of drug. In my professional opinion, for what it's worth, he was murdered. Most people don't choose to take their own life in their own home using this drug. It's used more for assisted suicides in Switzerland as it brings about a very reliable and peaceful death. But there is no evidence to prove that this was murder, the wine glass had only Jorey's prints on. Whoever did this to Jorey this was personal, if you like, a final act of kindness to take away his pain of loss and love, possibly.

There were other prints taken at the scene. I've been able to identify one set as Maggie Boscawen's, placing her in the art studio at some point. There was another set of abundant prints there, but so far, they haven't been identified.

There is a further breakthrough. Jorey's DNA matches the DNA found on Derwa Moon's body. Jorey Pomeroy was there at her death. The hairs that I found on her torso were from his head and would suggest they were planted on the body after her death, possibly to incriminate him.

The evidence isn't clear-cut for Jorey Pomeroy's death. All my experience leads me to conclude murder; however, the evidence discovered gives another story, and I will have to record Jorey Pomeroy's demise as attributed to death by misadventure.'

'Thanks Gilbert. Jorey Pomeroy must have had regular visitors to his workplace which will make it difficult to identify all the prints found, but not impossible if there is a link there and we are lucky. Placing him at Derwa Moon's death may be the reason why he was killed. He knew too much and was going to talk, if not now but eventually. They rarely stay silent for long.'

Everyone had something to hide Cornish thought. That was true of all human beings. Privacy was relational and depended on the audience, in this case, the police. Lying was an everyday social interaction, from small white lies to massive 'I didn't murder anyone' lies. This case was full of holes, and the one weak link in the chain had just been eliminated.

Cornish had the feeling that each one of the family members had more than a few skeletons in their closet.

Chapter Forty-One

Back at headquarters, the team were no further forward.

'We need evidence to back up any theory on a motive. From the very beginning if we take Lowenna Pascoe she, allegedly, drowned. My gut tells me she was murdered and if that was the case, then the suspect was Roger Pascoe. What was his motive?'

Mac piped up.
'His lover, Loveday. Either that or he hated his wife. No, I know, the money.'

Cornish continued.
'In Roger Pascoe's defence, I would suggest all three were equally strong motives. The only problem is that as he's dead, we will never really know the truth. And if Lowenna was murdered, then Roger is the obvious suspect. There was no sign of anybody else. Going on the autopsy from Gilbert we can't prove either way.

Next, Roger Pascoe was killed, shot, we know that much. It was by someone he knew, and who could handle guns. Whose footprints were on the ground by the kitchen window. Do we have a witness to the murder?

Maggie was strangled by someone with relatively small hands, and we believe she also knew the person. Her husband Steve has a motive, and his hands aren't significant. We know they'd had a row that morning. Did Steve Boscawen discover Maggie's affair and kill her? We know she was having a relationship with Jorey Pomeroy. Did Jorey kill her? If so why?

Now Jorey Pomeroy's dead. Who killed him? Was he murdered because someone thought he'd finished off Maggie, which puts Steve Boscawen back in the frame again? What about Barry Boscawen's actual father. Was he aware that he is Barry Boscawen's father? Did he kill Maggie? Does he live nearby? The fact that he was killed on 1 May, Beltaine Festival, also called Walpurgis Night is significant and where human sacrifice is required.'

Hutchens interrupted.

'We know Jorey picked Derwa up. He must have taken her to Bodmin Moor. Jorey Pomeroy was a member of the Satanic cult group? The link back to the Pascoe family is Maggie and Paul Hicks.'

The list was getting longer, not shorter. Agreed, the suspects were dwindling, but that was assuming one of them was their killer or if there were multiple killers. The arrows on the whiteboard crisscrossed to each of the remaining family members. It was time to bring in the big guns and interview the remaining family under caution. Cornish had played by the rules. Now they needed to finish this and catch the killer or killers. The stakes were high and the prize even higher to the last man or woman standing.

'We can't fuck this up.'

The family members had assisted the police with their enquires voluntarily, but now she had to bring them all back under caution to use any further answers, or silence in court.

246

How many times in her career had she said the words? 'You do not have to say anything. But it may harm your defence if you do not mention when questioned, something which you later rely on in court. Anything you do say may be given in evidence.' Too many.

The problem was that Cornish had no firm evidence to link any one of them directly to the murders except Jorey's DNA and he was dead. There was no half-way house. Attending the police station voluntarily the person was free to leave unless arrested. They could be cautioned, questioned and still allowed to leave. Cornish needed reasonable grounds for suspecting that one of them had committed or was going to commit, an offence.

Cornish knew from Clemo Nicholl that the estate Administration was yet to be completed. There was a war going on which from where Cornish was looking was about to get bloodier.

Chapter Forty-Two

Cornish knew from her experience that killers could seem normal to the outside world. They were neighbours, friends, family, parents and peers in every sense of the word. They went to church, had common jobs and even participated in community life. Anybody who took a quick glance at their lives would see nothing out of the ordinary. But take a more in-depth look, and you'd see a dark, sinister person lurking underneath the mask of normality. These men and women took pleasure in killing others. Cornish was convinced Hicks was the killer. She suspected he could be quite kind when the mood suited him, and he was handsome and charismatic, calm, friendly and a well-spoken guy. He loved his mother. He was a chameleon with many faces. Smart and self-aware, a cocky bastard. One of the few killers that wouldn't turn himself in.

There were no coincidences or accidents rather chain reactions of cause and effect manifesting on the physical plane interpreted by the law of opposites: likes or dislikes, pleasure or pain. Cornish was the light as Paul Hicks was the darkness and the one thing Cornish realised was not to glorify the dark side. Paul Hicks believed that Satan would help give him the power to recreate his future. Cornish would make sure, along with her team, that didn't happen. Too many had already died for this maniac in her eyes. The more the team read up on Satanic rituals, the more they realised just how much importance it meant to the leader of this group.

There were now only four members of the family left alive, Nadine Pascoe and her two children Emma and Paul and Barry Boscawen. Steve Boscawen didn't stand to inherit from Maggie although Cornish hadn't ruled out the possibility that he could have killed Maggie. Jorey Pomeroy was dead, Maggie's lover and part of the Satanic Cult headed by Paul Hicks. And this was the crux of the investigation Cornish, and her team couldn't point the finger at Hicks for Maggie's death. His alibi was rock solid. At the time of Maggie Pascoe's murder, Paul Hicks was on the other coast. Neither could they produce the evidence to link him to the deaths of Sonny, Derwa, Finley and Jorey. Peter Chegwin had confessed to his part, but without further corroboration, they had insufficient findings to present to the Crown Prosecution Service (CPS).

Cornish leaned back in her chair allowing the irritation to seep out of her system before she spoke. She was getting tired of the daily trudge of dealing with the scum of the earth yet without this in her life there would be a void. She had no family waiting for her at home, Englebert was her only companion. Policing was her life. Jane Falconbridge had offered her the position of Detective Chief Superintendent vacancy, but Cornish didn't want a desk job either. What kept her awake at night was the fact that the likes of Paul Hicks continued to be free when they should be locked up for life and the key discarded. The cell was once again empty, and a killer was on the loose and Cornish knew who would be next to die.

Chapter Forty-Three

Peter Chegwin picked up the phone. He had remained locked in his home for days since confessing to the police about his participation in the murders. Somehow the press had got wind of the story, and they now stood outside his bungalow waiting to catch a glimpse of him or an opportunity to get his side of the story. The butcher's shop was now a crime scene. SOCO had examined the premises but come away with nothing. He could have told them that, he did, but they hadn't believed him. Peter Chegwin was if nothing scrupulously clean with his instruments and the disposal of the ABP. His job was finished, and his neighbours shunned him. He had become a pariah overnight.

Hicks wanted to meet up. He explained that he would make sure Peter didn't take the blame for anything. Hicks was prepared to take the rap, but they needed to get their stories straight before he handed himself over to the police. Hicks suggested meeting in Padstow to make Peter feel secure. The place was a tourist trap and would be brimming with visitors. Peter didn't think Hicks would try anything there. Foolishly he agreed.

He managed to sneak out the back of his property and slip away without being tailed by any of the media.
Peter Chegwin parked his van in the public pay and display car park.
He walked over to the harbour and sat down on the bench waiting for Hicks to turn up. Hicks had spotted him and was casually sauntering towards him with various pieces of kit in his arms, a rucksack and some fishing rods. He had a boat in the harbour and was restocking for a fishing trip. Hicks handed Chegwin some of the gear, and he proceeded to follow him like a lamb to the slaughter. Amongst the visitors, he naively thought Hicks would be foolish to attempt to harm him. I guess the moral of the story is don't do stupid shit and follow a killer into his lair no matter how public it appears. Chegwin actively chose to risk his life, oblivious to the fact that it would lead to his death.

Hicks handed a beer to Chegwin as he unpacked his supplies casually discussing his forthcoming plans for the Satanic Cult. He made no mention of his detainment in the police cells or the fact that Chegwin had confirmed him as the Grand Master.

Hicks started the engine, and before Chegwin had a chance to object, they were chugging out of the inner harbour heading out into open water. Chegwin could feel the cold starting to creep into his body, his palms sweating, his heart picking up the pace and the chill finally materialising into anxiety. He hadn't dressed for the weather. They reached a point, and Hicks killed the switch on the engine. They were bobbing around. Hicks motioned to Chegwin to pass him the rope by his feet, and as Chegwin knelt down to pick up it up Hicks pushed him into the cold Atlantic Sea. Chegwin surprised gulped in the salty water as the hard, impossible waves, pounded him. The curious thing was that Chegwin didn't realise he was going to die much earlier.

Terrified out of his mind he didn't have any air to breathe. He couldn't get out of the water, escape. Afraid for his life he didn't want to die, not in this way. He grasped for the boat, but he was unable to grab hold. Paul Hicks just watched, his face showing no emotion at all. The feeling of utter certainty, knowing he was going to die came over Peter so severely that he honestly didn't know how at that moment his body didn't go into shock. Instead, the crushing piercing inevitability of his death was so grave there was no room for sanity. The violent struggle with the elements was proving too much. Hicks admired the fight in Chegwin and felt almost privileged to witness his death. Chegwin didn't surrender easily as he began to lose consciousness intermittently. He kept swimming, kicking his legs frantically, desperate for air as he was churned around until he no longer knew up from down. The current relaxed its grip then another wave pushed him back under battering and winding him. Out of his depth, he struggled, an intense pain bloomed at the top of his chest, spreading downwards and inwards, his lungs giving out or his heart until eventually he accepted death and the sea pulled him under and then everything went black.

Paul Hicks wasn't affected by Peter Chegwin's drowning. He respected the man for putting up a fight as the sea claimed its latest victim. He had fought well. Many tourists had drowned in the riptides of the North Atlantic coast, and Peter Chegwin would be another fatality attributed to the dangerous waters. The waves had become choppier as the afternoon eased into the evening and Peter Chegwin's body had disappeared.

Hicks restarted the engine and chugged back towards the harbour on the tide. No one noticed the little boat had gone out and returned. The tourists were oblivious to the comings and goings in the port, and the fishermen were too busy with their catches and making money. Paul Hicks sloped off back to his home, and no one was none the wiser. None of the family was aware that he even had a boat and somethings were better-kept secrets. Two of his group were dead.

Four could now keep a secret if three of them were dead.

Chapter Forty-Four

The bloated body washed up on Perranporth beach three weeks later and was discovered by local dog walkers. It was a small place to find a dead body on the beach and the police buzzing around was not an everyday thing. SOCO arrived along with Cornish and her team.

The sea had done its worst along with the rocks and the sand abrasions. A few fish and crabs and crustaceans had nibbled at the exposed parts of the body, fingers, the soft parts of the face like the eyes and lips which had been in the water for three weeks. A body on the open ocean where flies and other insects were mostly absent and floating in water less than 21 degrees Celsius started to become bloated with the skin blistering and turning greenish black. The tissues had transformed into a soapy fatty acid known as grave wax that halted bacterial growth. The body after this length of time was highly decomposed and would only be identified through DNA analysis or dental records. Mac looked at the figure and felt his stomach turn. Even in the open air, the stench was strong.

Pearce and Mac walked the beach looking for any clues and talked to the locals. No one had been reported missing. Cornish and Hutchens checked the missing person's database but judging by the state of the corpse they would have to wait for Gilbert to complete his report.

The body was transported back to Gilbert who had the enviable task of dissecting it and establishing the cause of death and identity. Gilbert unwrapped the corpse enthusiastically. He could honestly say he enjoyed his job. Every day was different and every corpse unique in their own special way.

The human body, specifically a human corpse had a rank and pungent smell mixed with a tinge of sickening sweetness. Imagine a rotting piece of meat with a couple of drops of cheap perfume, and you would be halfway to what a human corpse smelled like.

The smell dispersed rapidly from the carcass or whether it was just that Gilbert was used to the smell after all these years and didn't use anything to mask it. You got used to anything in the end but the worse was opening up an abdomen at necropsy and nicking the bowel and it literally exploding in your face which he had done before. The rule was never to smile when opening the gut, you were worrying about the wrong thing focusing on the smell. Really rank ones were rare.

Regardless of the composition of water Gilbert had to establish the fact of whether the person drowned as a result of misadventure or murder before going into the water or not. The body had surpassed the initial stages of external froth which had been washed away by the sea. There was no doubt the body was waterlogged in the lungs due to the pleural fluid accumulation. The middle ear was congested as were the solid organs such as the liver and there were muscular haemorrhages in the neck and back indicating signs of drowning. Microscopy revealed nothing conclusive and the diatom testing was considered ubiquitous as was the specific gravity analysis. However, the blood strontium analysis proved to a reasonable degree of certainty that this male had drowned in seawater.

Cornish and Hutchens turned up for the results. The investigation was going nowhere fast, and they had lost a prime witness, Peter Chegwin. His neighbours hadn't seen him for three weeks, and Cornish suspected that their floater was Chegwin which wouldn't help their case against Hicks.

Gilbert, as usual, rambled on.
'This body had definitely spent time sleeping with fishes. Not a pleasant job considering mere moments after death body decomposition kicked in as the bacterial enzymes started to break down the body's soft tissues and blood vessels. From there a pretty predictable process of putrefaction, followed by bloating, purging, advanced decay and finally dry remains, unless at sea. However, being submerged in water stopped the buffet from flies and other creepy crawlies. This body wasn't a floater which

helped me determine that he was not murdered before being entering the water. Fortunately, the body breaks down more slowly in the open air. A body putrefies faster in warmer stagnant or fresh water than in cold salty running water. Needless to say, being submerged in water caused the epidermis to blister and turn greenish-black and the skin to become swollen, bleached and wrinkled as you can see. The submerged corpse decaying underwater developed a build-up of bacteria in the gut and chest cavity to produce methane, carbon dioxide and hydrogen sulphide – gas. The result is that the torso rose first, and the head and limbs dangled behind which is why floaters are normally face down in the water. The body has been preserved by the Adipocere, the hard-waxy greyish substance that forms during decomposition. This male was intact, but it's not unusual for hands and feet to break off the body first. DNA was the only way to identify this man. Your dead body is one Peter Chegwin and his death was attributed to drowning. Sorry, Cornish, I know you wanted this to be murder, but there are no contusions on the body to suggest assault from my examination and any bruising and damage can be attributed to the Atlantic Ocean beating the hell out of him.'

Gilbert quickly covered the body to prevent further odours from seeping into their skin. He opened the bank of metal draws lined along the one wall and using the metal gurney he slid the body back into its allotted place and closed the door.

The only thing that was going to remove the stench of death would be getting justice for the victims and catching the killer.

Chapter Forty-Five

'Another dead end. Smug bastard. Hicks might think he's one step ahead of us, but the net is closing in.'

It wasn't often Cornish lost her rag.

'Before we bring in Hicks let's give him enough rope to hang himself. I want the rest of the Pascoe family brought in for questioning. No one singled out, and no one left out. Someone must know something. Anything they say might seem meaningless to them but could be of great importance to us cracking this case. Pearce and Mac, you bring in Eddy Hicks, and we'll bring in Steve Boscawen. Let's see what these two men have to say about their wives and family.

Eddy Hicks sat in one interview room while Steve Boscawen sat in another. Of the two men, Steve was the most nervous. Clemo Nicholl accompanied Steve Boscawen as he was still considered part of the family and Barry had insisted his father be represented in-house. Cornish and Hutchens sat opposite, and Cornish recited the standard caution for the benefit of the audio tape and Boscawen. Clemo Nicholl had advised his client to say nothing but Steve couldn't just sit there and keep his mouth shut. The pressure of just being in the police interview room was causing him to perspire excessively. The room felt oppressively hot, and his heart inside his chest was beating like a drum in a gallop rhythm. He suspected that he wouldn't be sitting here if the police had nothing. The questioning started with his name and address and where he was residing. They were increasing the pressure notch by notch. Hutchens spoke the most while Cornish watched observing every single voluntary or involuntary movement Boscawen made. They wanted to analyse every minute detail leading up to Maggie's death. Steve's head was pounding after a couple of hours. It was difficult enough to remember what he had done yesterday let alone the events and the argument that had culminated in their fight the night before Maggie was murdered. He maintained his innocence throughout the first two hours. Cornish and Hutchens left him with his solicitor while they took a short break. The afternoon session would be the ball breaker.

Meanwhile, Pearce and Mac had been in with Eddy Hicks. He'd declined legal representation. He was a nutcase, two bricks short of a loaf. Hardwired and from a poorer neighbourhood Pearce couldn't believe he had been married to Nadine. She had chosen to marry a bit of rough in her younger days, probably to annoy the hell out of her family. Eddy Hicks had been bought up the hard way where a good slap had never done anyone any harm, and he had the boxer's nose to show he had been in a fair few fights in his youth. His demeanour was one of having been there, done that and spent time in the cells. His record detailed several times in youth detention for GBH but nothing more serious. He wasn't in the habit of slapping women around and the last time he'd seen Nadine was at his daughter Emma's birthday bash. Pearce questioned Hicks about his whereabouts on the morning Maggie died, and his alibi was checked out by Mac. Eddy Hicks had been at work, his shift pattern had been early with plenty of witnesses.

'I told you where I was. Why the hell would I want to kill Maggie?'

'Weren't you and Maggie an item years ago?'

'Look, I've got nothing to hide. Maggie and I used to fuck. She fucked a lot of blokes and then she got pregnant. I don't know who the father was, Maggie wouldn't say. Then we split up, and I went out with Nadine. Maggie lost the baby, that's all I know and then a while later we started occasionally fucking, but that was all. Nadine was a frigid bitch, even back then. Maggie married Steve Boscawen. We'd still meet up, and then one day Maggie said she was pregnant, and it was mine. I didn't want a kid back then. Maggie and I didn't see each other after that except at family do's and Nadine never knew as far as I am aware. Why the fuck would I say anything. As far as I was concerned Barry was Steve's son, not mine. He brought him up.'

Pearce relayed the interview to Cornish during the break.

'Release Eddy Hicks. He's not our man. He may be many things, but he's not our killer.'

Eddy Hicks walked out of the Police Station a free man.

'Fuck you, Steve Boscawen.'

The afternoon session started with going over the pre-emptive 999 calls made by Steve Boscawen to the police stating that something was wrong as Frank their dog was on the drive without Maggie.

'Why did you assume something was wrong because not getting hold of someone right away is pretty normal?' replied Cornish.

'I don't know.'

Cornish played the call Steve Boscawen had placed to the police that morning.

'I really loved her. We were happily married.'

His tone was all wrong. He was too calm, lucid, not hysterical as he would have been in that situation.

'Mr Boscawen, I would understand if you and Maggie had a fight and it got out of hand. Is that what happened?'

'I swear on my mother's grave that I didn't kill her.'

That was Boscawen's second mistake. An innocent person would usually answer with a direct yes or no. Those involved were more likely to give a long answer as a way of stalling.

'Look, I explained to the police when I called why I was concerned. I loved Maggie, and we were happy, so I didn't know why she had disappeared. I told you we'd had a silly argument, but that was all it was.'

Boscawen was hanging himself. Too many details, his story was carefully planned to anticipate what he would be asked. Too many inconsistencies in his innocuous statement. Lying about the small stuff.

He had referred to Maggie in the past-tense on the 999 calls. Most people held out some hope that their missing wife would be found alive, but Boscawen had referred to her in the past tense.

'Did you kill Maggie, Steve? By mistake?'

'Huh.'

'You heard me' repeated Cornish.

'I don't know what you mean. I loved Maggie.'

Steve held his head in his hands and wept.

'Someone else hurt my Maggie. Why aren't you out there looking for them? What about Eddy Hicks. He had sex with Maggie and Barry was, after all, his son.'

This was Boscawen's next mistake. Offering a helpful other explanation and shifting the suspicion to another person.

'Eddy Hicks has a solid alibi.'

'How did you feel when you found out Barry was Eddy Hicks, son?'

'How do you think. Angry, hurt but I would never hurt Maggie. She was my wife, and I loved her.'

Cornish decided to change tact.

'How did you feel when you found out about Jorey?'

Steve Boscawen looked up, and it was as if a switch had been flicked. Anger and hatred seeped from every pore, and he scowled at Jorey Pomeroy's name.

'That bastard never loved Maggie like me. He was just a fuck buddy, nothing more.'

'Except that Maggie had told you the night before that she was leaving you for Jorey and that made you angry. My guess is you knew exactly where Maggie was going that morning, and you caught up with her on her way home and killed her.'

'No, no, no. I loved Maggie.'

'Enough to kill her?'

'Yes, no. Oh god, what have I done? She was so beautiful, my Maggie. She wouldn't listen. Oh god.'

Steve Boscawen wept like a baby as Cornish said.

'Book him.'

Boscawen had destroyed himself with his own confession. Hutchens completed the statement and Steve Boscawen, a broken man, was led away to the cells. They had one result. Maggie Boscawen's murder had been solved. One down. The other deaths would not be so easy. Not counting Lowenna Pascoe there were five more murders to solve.

Chapter Forty-Six

Barry Boscawen sat in the interview room angry and pissed off. His father had murdered his mother. That useless bastard had been a waste of space as a father and as a husband all his life. It was no surprise to him that she'd had many affairs. He'd heard through the grapevine of local gossip about his mother putting it about but as long as she was happy, he hadn't cared. His mother had more intelligence in her little toe than his father had in his small brain. As far as Barry was concerned his dad was a drunk and always would be.

Clemo Nicholls sat once more beside his client. His law practice was getting plenty of media attention. Any publicity was better than no publicity as far as he was concerned. Once again, he conferred with Barry and advised him to assist the police with their enquires. Barry Boscawen wanted his pound of flesh. He wanted his inheritance which he had been denied and as far as he was concerned whoever was killing off the Pascoe family was doing him a favour. Providing he lived to get his share.

The questioning commenced, and this time Pearce took the lead with Cornish observing. She didn't like Barry Boscawen. He considered himself a notch above the rest of society. It was evident that Barry hated his family and had minimal regard for women. He had adored his mother. The rest of them could rot in hell.

'Look, I don't know what you want me to tell you. I haven't killed anyone. Yes, I hated my grandfather for what he did to my mother. I can't say I like the others much. They are all in it for the money. None of them put in as much effort as I do when it comes to increasing family wealth. I am the only one who ever does a full day's work. So, yes, I'm pissed, pissed that I have to be part of this family and all its shit.'

'What size shoe are you?' Cornish interrupted.

'A ten. Why?'

'What were you doing at Roger Pascoe's on the night he was murdered?'

Barry hadn't been expecting that. How had the bitch known? Someone must have seen him. It was pointless to deny it if that was the case. It would only put him in the frame for the other murders. He needed to think quickly. Actually, what was the point? They were the police, and if he knew anything at all from all the crime series on television, the police knew when a suspect was lying. It was better, to tell the truth, no matter how bad it looked.

'Okay, I was there. Is that what you wanted to hear. I had gone over to confront the old man, and yes, I would have loved to have killed him. I didn't. I was too late. When I got there, I parked in the layby away from the farmhouse. The kitchen light was on, and the engine of my grandfather's Landy was warm, so I assumed he was still up. Then I heard the shot as I walked towards the farmhouse. I stood still for a few minutes. Then the door opened, so I quickly ducked down and hid in the shadow of the bushes. I couldn't make out who it was. He looked around, I thought he might have heard me, but he turned back, locked the door and walked off down the lane. When he'd disappeared out of sight, I crept up and peered in through the window. My grandfather was sitting slumped in the kitchen chair with his face blown off. He looked dead to me; I didn't go inside. And I don't have a key. That's all I know. Yes, I should have called the police. I didn't. Let's face it, it didn't look good from where I was standing, and he was dead. So, I left. I knew he would be found in the morning by his cleaner. You can't book me for that?'

By the time they had finished questioning Barry Boscawen, they were no nearer to the truth. Barry had seen his grandfather's killer, and if Pearce and Cornish's assessment of the situation was correct, it could only be Paul Hicks who had killed him. Barry had described the person as a male, but that could just have been a turn of speech. Nevertheless, Paul Hicks was in the frame, and the last man left. The others had already been dismissed from their enquires or were dead. The problem was Cornish still had no concrete proof. She needed a confession.

Barry Boscawen walked out of the police headquarters a free man, but the killer was still out there.

Not for long if Cornish had anything to do with it. The net was closing in and fast.

Chapter Forty-Seven

Nadine Pascoe sat expressionless opposite Cornish and Hutchens. She denied legal representation wanting to send a clear message to her interrogators. Nadine had no alibi for the times in question citing that she was at home alone and there were no witnesses. Cornish questioned her about her childhood. Nadine was a closed book. She had revealed very little of herself before when interviewed informally in her home in Truro. The only glimmer of information was of Barry Boscawen's biological father, Eddy Hicks.

As far as Nadine was concerned it was nobody else's business what had happened. She was just eight years old when the abuse started, and it had continued into her teens. She would take that with her to her grave. The events had already taken her to some very dark places along with the discovery of her father's secrets.

Nadine and Maggie had often talked about their childhood and being victims of their father's actions many times. He should have been their provider, their protector. Instead, he violated them. Nadine felt that her family were secondary crime victims, still carrying a lot of the shame, Nadine more so.

If Nadine knew anything about her son, she wasn't saying. Cornish broached Nadine about her relationship with her father.

'Knowing my father caused pain to my mother caused me pain. Do you think he killed her DCI Cornish?'

Cornish couldn't answer that except to say what the evidence revealed. Nadine already knew why her father had killed her mother. It was because he could. He was a monster.

Nadine had learned the truth about her father as a teenager and eventually found a way to live with it. Only once had she attempted to articulate her feelings to a school counsellor, but it hadn't come out right. After that, she didn't bother again.

Her father had made her feel uncomfortable as a young woman. He had been sexually explicit and graphic when her mother wasn't around and would leer at women in public, make lewd remarks about them and occasionally harass them, flirting horribly with them.

Nadine had felt dirty, less of a person, isolated. It was as if she was a spectator, watching ordinary people in a world go about their lives. Anyone looking in saw only the trappings of a wealthy family, not the dysfunctional one. Nadine coped with the events by compartmentalising her life, for her own sanity. Eventually, she left the family home but ended up going out with boys who were violent and abusive. Then Nadine met Eddy Hicks. She thought he would be different. It turned out that he couldn't keep his dick in his pants. She had Paul and Emma before managing to extricate herself from the marriage. Nadine knew her father had molested her children and hated him all the more. She had been unable to protect them.

Maggie hadn't been subjected to the same level of abuse as Nadine and Barry had been left alone. Nadine resented Maggie for that and had mixed emotions for her ranging from a sisterly closeness to insatiable anger at times. Why had her family been mistreated, and Maggie's son left alone?

Nadine still believed up to a certain point in her life that her father had loved her and her children, that he was capable of love and empathy. Then one day he told her that he had harboured thoughts of killing her and her children. Finally, Nadine knew the answer to the question that had been bothering her every time she thought about their last meal together. Would he have killed her if she had told the police about him? Yes, he would. Understanding that allowed Nadine to say goodbye to him. He had deserved to die. Her loyalty was to her own family, and she would have carried their secrets to her grave if circumstances had been different.
Turning to Satanism had allowed her to acknowledge the pain and anger she felt and channel it through this belief.

Satanism taught her to love herself at the expense of others. The darkness had gripped her. Their leader, her son, had embraced the Eleven Satanic Rules of the Earth to the extreme. He had gone too far. The terrible nightmares started, and Nadine knew that Satan would not be her salvation. Maggie had tried to convert Nadine back to the church and traditional Christianity but extricating herself from the group would be impossible. They were her family.

Everyone had a period of denial, where they rode the pendulum of shock and grief deluding themselves. Then came the anger. Nadine had denied herself her rightful position for too long. She had allowed her unconditional love for her offspring to conceal what they really were. It was her womb that had brought them into the world, and it would be her that delivered them to the gates of hell.

Cornish regarded Nadine. While she displayed empathy for those murdered Cornish was convinced Nadine was masking her real self. Cornish knew both Paul and Emma had been abused as children by their grandfather, yet Nadine had not disclosed this information. She had clammed up.

Cornish and Hutchens watched Nadine Pascoe gaze at the four walls. With her arms crossed she eventually looked Cornish in the eye.

'No comment.'

After several hours of trying to extract any conversation from Nadine Cornish and Hutchens retreated to consider their next move. There was no evidence linking Nadine Pascoe to the murders and if Nadine knew anything, she wasn't going to tell them.

Nadine walked out of the police headquarters and smiled. She hadn't given the police what they wanted. Her silence would only protect her for so long.

Chapter Forty-Eight

Cornish and her team had spent several months combing through evidence, re-tracing police work and trying to get people to talk. Nadine Pascoe had revealed nothing new in the investigation; she was hiding something. Emma Hicks would be the next to be brought in for formal questioning. Then they got lucky. A video podcast had appeared and was being aired on the internet, and someone recognised Paul Hicks or his doppelgänger. He was the only one of the Satanic Cult group clearly visible offering Finley Jago up to Satan. Cornish looked carefully at the film; something was glistening on one of the other member's fingers, a ring perhaps. She would get their IT guy Dave to cast his trained eye on the podcast.

One of the group members must have filmed the ritual. If Paul Hicks was aware of the existence of this podcast, then it would undoubtedly be a reason for killing off the other members. It wasn't pleasant viewing, and Jane Falconbridge ordered the podcast to be removed from public display. It would do their case no good and would only further public animosity towards the police and the last thing she wanted was a witch hunt for Paul Hicks.

Cornish was livid.

'I want Paul Hicks in the dock of a criminal court, accused of these murders dressed in his best suit to face the legal fight of his life. He might well profess his innocence, but you and I know fine well he's a murderer and this now proves that beyond any doubt in my book. The problem will be the jury of twelve men and women selected from the community, people who will have been following the case and may have read the scandalous crimes committed but will have also read this man claiming he has been set up and is innocent and this wasn't him in the podcast. Without a confession, we are relying on the jury to either free Hicks or imprison him for years, hopefully, the remainder of his life. But, we need a solid confession to ensure the jury make the right choice or at the very least the person who made this podcast. How often have the jury got it wrong? You and I both know the decision can go either way. We can't afford to make any mistakes. Our case against Hicks and anyone else for that matter must be watertight.'

Jane Falconbridge agreed with Cornish, but they had to play by the rules. Cornish was looking forward to getting Hicks into court. The police wouldn't have a say on the judge, but if Cornish had her pick, she would choose Judge Barbara Smith to deliberate on the fate of Hicks and whether he was guilty of the following deaths: Roger Pascoe, Finley Jago, Jorey Pomeroy, Sonny the horse, Derwa Moon and Peter Chegwin. Cornish was well aware of how juries made their judgements about the person on trial, and it would surprise the average citizen.

Hicks could request a trial by jury rather than a judge only trial citing the reason that he was unlikely to get a fair trial because the case had been covered in the media. He would be hoping for a retrial with the jury or an acquittal. Juries were swayed by many different factors which were not always logical and reasonable. The judge would be less likely to be influenced by what had been reported in the media. There was no doubt that physical appearance, religious beliefs and race or ethnicity swayed juries. And a well-spoken public schoolboy educated posh knob would look good on the stand and Cornish knew he would be able to convince the best of them that he was innocent. The judge may instruct the jury not to read the media coverage of the trial or listen to gossip or discuss the trial with people outside the jury room, but that was not realistic. It was a big ask especially when it was someone's ten minutes of fame.

Judges were trained as lawyers, and this training and experience made it relatively easy to decide whether a person was guilty or not guilty beyond reasonable doubt. Juries didn't understand the phrase. The law wasn't always fair and just. A client who had major public backing or sympathy and was well-known and liked was less likely to be convicted because of his status as a respected public figure. It might be poppycock, but it was the truth.

If Hicks insisted on a plea of not guilty with a jury the police might get lucky and win. If he confessed to committing the crimes and insisted on going to trial Clemo Nicholl would have the pleasure of defending him without a positive defence. Cornish wouldn't want to be in his shoes. The trial would be one big final circus.

Cornish thought carefully about their options. Finally, she addressed her team.
'I want Paul, and Emma Hicks picked up. Something tells me they are both in this together.'

Pearce and Mac drove to Emma Hicks place in Truro while Cornish and Hutchens drove to Padstow. Neither were at home. Both places appeared deserted which begged the question of where was Emma and Paul Hicks? An alert was put out for both vehicles, and it was several hours later that a call was patched through to Cornish.
This time Cornish would catch her killer.

Chapter Forty-Nine

Most lighthouses were in secluded spots, and this one was no different. There were no neighbours, bar the cormorants and shags and nothing overlooking it except the cliffs. The car park was the National Trust car park five minutes away, and visitors had to walk down a 300m path to get to Sailors Watch Cottage. The network of public footpaths led from the lighthouse gate around the headland cliffs to an old gun battery and a little-used swimming beach for the cottage next to the working lighthouse. St Anthony's Lighthouse stood on the eastern side of the entrance to Carrick Roads, one of the largest natural harbours in the world.

When it came to mysterious lighthouses, St Anthony's had enough ghosts and curses and sudden deaths over the years. It had been in the Pascoe family for what seemed an eternity and sat snugly at the end of the peninsula atop a lonely rocky outlet routinely battered by waves. It had a dark history.

The solitary, isolated whitewashed cottage used to be the family home for the lighthouse keeper and his family. Before that, it was used in wartime by the Territorial Army responsible for the defence of Carrick Roads during the Second World War. The lighthouse was commissioned to warn the ships of the presence of the Mannacles, a dangerous crescent of hazardous rocks in the middle of the channel said to have sunk plenty of passing ships attempting to navigate the waters into the harbour.

A storm had been brewing, and Cornish hoped it wasn't a bad omen. They walked from the car park up the overgrown path to the lighthouse and cottage. By the time the team reached there, they were drenched. Storm Hector, the most powerful summer gale in almost thirty years had arrived, as predicted, bringing gale force winds and rain to the south of the country. The sea was violently crashing against the rocks, and the buildings and St Mawes was barely visible through the spray. The ocean's fury was battering the coastline causing the waves to attain great heights as it smashed against the structures. The Spring tides would only increase the severity of the storm and Cornwall had been bracing itself for the full force.

Dusk lent everything a supernatural quality and Cornish banged on the private property's solid oak door. There was life inside and a light burned and flickered with the weather. She could hear raised voices. Emma and Paul Hicks were inside shouting, and Cornish didn't think they had heard the door. Cornish considered the foreboding Carrick Roads would be an existential environment for someone to die.

Inside the cottage, furniture was being thrown and smashed as Emma held her brother at bay. Paul leapt over a table lunging at her. He wanted her dead. She had betrayed him, and the bitch was going to pay. Emma laughed at his feeble attempts to grab her and restrain her. The scuffle was not going to plan.

'I don't believe you. How could you do it?' yelled Paul.

'This is over. We're done. You killed them all.' Emma taunted him. She had heard the banging on the door. She had staged the whole thing assuming that it wouldn't take the police long to track their whereabouts.

'How dare you! How dare you, he yelled. You can't run away. You killed him, didn't you?'

Glaring at her brother she was ready to set up the finale. Emma's diabolical, twisted mind had conjured up the scenario for this last act. And no one would ever know the truth, except for her. This would be a fitting end.
'You are an evil poison, a psychopath who needs permanent confinement. You certainly won't fool a jury of your peers. You're a disgrace to humanity and a plague on society.'

'I pray that the truth will prevail you evil cow.'
Paul was in no mood for games.

'You won't fool anyone Paul, sitting in a courtroom.'

Something wasn't right. The cottage suddenly went quiet. Rather than proceeding through the front door Cornish instructed Pearce and Mac to circle around the path to see if there was another entrance to the cottage. A minute later Pearce opened the front door, and Cornish and Hutchens stepped inside. There was no one there.

'It looks as if they ran out from the other door' replied Pearce.

The small fire was petering out in the grate, and the cottage felt suddenly cold. Cornish peered from the window to see two figures running along the coastal path. Then there was the unmistakable sound of a gunshot in the direction Cornish was looking. Cornish sprinted out of the door towards the coastal track followed by the rest of her team. She wasn't the fittest, rather more carthorse than racehorse and on the coastal pathway, she had to tread carefully as there was no barrier to stop her from falling. The track was rocky and the going unsteady given the weather and the light. She switched the light on her mobile to help see the path ahead.

Meanwhile, Paul was chasing Emma, his long legs tearing up the ground. Emma was like a whippet as her heart hammered against her chest as she pushed herself to run faster to distance herself from her brother. She glanced back but couldn't see him through the rain and spray. Where was he?

Paul had stopped dead still, listening, trying to gauge where Emma was. Had she slipped off the path or ran off inland to get help at one of the other cottages occupied by holidaymakers. He didn't think so. He laughed at the situation as the darkness closed in. He continued on the path taking the chance that Emma would try to hide in one of the coves on one of the three beaches nearby.
Dangerous but stupid with storm Hector. As children, they had played on the beaches many times and knew the caves well.

Cornish was ahead when she heard another gunshot disturbing a flock of resting birds. There was no time to waste. The failing light and the driving rain cast a depressing lack of hope in finding Emma and Paul in one piece if they didn't hurry. Cornish frequently stopped to listen for the sound of footfall and thought she heard the faintish sound of feet running up ahead.

Hutchens was right behind her boss. Mac and Pearce were coming up the rear, Pearce cursing the last time he had done any physical activity.

Emma had no idea of distance or direction in the storm. She only knew she had to get away. She was soaked to the skin and freezing. She had run out of the cottage without her coat which would have only held her pace back as it was heavy. She was regretting that decision. The warmth would have been better than the possibility of hypothermia from the weather. As she glanced back, she saw the glare of the lights on the lighthouse. She could make out a shadow. Paul was gaining on her all the time, and she felt her legs slowing down. Paul had the one and only gun, and she knew he intended to use it if he got the chance. She had to get into the caves, but she couldn't be sure which beach she was running down to. There were three beaches accessible from the path, the first, great Molunan beach was sandy with a small cove, then there was Little Molunan beach which was smaller, rockier, and the last beach had no name, this cave was the largest against the steep cliff path, the most difficult to access but offered her the best protection. Emma descended the trail which was unstable and slippery. She fell backwards several times and glided down the last bit onto the beach with no name. The waves were smashing up onto what was left of the beach, and Emma knew it would be only a matter of time before it would be inaccessible.

Cornish moved quickly along the path, her thighs burning, cursing her lack of fitness lately. She was almost there. She could make out Paul ahead before he disappeared off to the left. Cornish halted when she reached the same spot and waited for Hutchens Mac and Pearce to catch up.

'They are down there somewhere. Be careful. Pearce, stop here at the top just in case they double back.'

They stepped forward and looked down the steep path. They were better and safer on higher ground. And Cornish knew one of them had a gun. Cornish requested backup. She turned to the youngest protégé Mac and instructed him to go back to the cottage and wait for the response team.
'Hutchens and I will go down.'
She jabbed a finger towards the cave's entrance, a darker and ominous

shadow 'That's where they'll be.'

Cornish and Hutchens started their careful descent down the path which was being washed away by the storm.
'Make sure the coastguard is on alert. We may just need their help to get back up.'

Carrick Roads was renowned for its fair share of deaths from falls or drowning. Cornish didn't know which was the better way to die, and she didn't want to find out.

Emma laid face down on the rocky beach. She must have tripped and fallen unconscious for a couple of minutes, her body giving in to the stress and exhaustion, after her desperate flight from the cottage. Pain ricocheted through her body as Emma realised, she had been shot in the leg by Paul. She was cold, sore and her jeans were blood-soaked. She struggled to her feet and tried to move towards the edge of the cave away from the approaching tide. The cave was dark, and a menacing moment of fear made her tremble. It was hopeless. Then she heard a voice, one she had hoped to never hear again.

'Emma!'

Paul was behind her.

'Emma!'

Paul stood with his back to the sea. He raised the gun and was about to fire when Cornish threw herself towards him knocking him off balance and into the rocky waters.

Winded and bruised Cornish stood up with Hutchens help. Paul was on his feet again, only just, struggling to stand up as the waves were racing towards the shore. Cornish was face-to-face with a rabid dog; his gun claimed by the sea. Paul laughed and shouted.

'I'm going to miss our little chats.'

'Really? I don't think there is anywhere to go from here except behind bars where you belong.'

'That's not going to happen.'

Paul Hicks took a step back, then another.

'That's far enough,' Cornish shouted.

'I don't think so.'

'Get out of the sea' shouted Cornish.

'The entire place is surrounded by police. You can't escape. It's over.'

Paul Hicks was angry. No one got the better of him.

'I think not.'

Hicks walked backwards into the sea with the waves crashing into him. Another few steps and he would be swept out and battered against the Mannacles. Cornish watched unable to convince him to give himself up as he reared up and threw himself across the waves. For a fleeting moment, he regretted his impulsive decision as he struggled to remain afloat. His body thrashed against the water as his lungs screamed for air and finally, he allowed the sea to take him to his death.

Emma Hicks was shaking violently from the cold and the excitement of watching her brother take his own life. Cornish misinterpreted her reaction as fear. Emma gave a self-deprecating laugh, then surveyed Cornish with a measure of pity. Cornish would never understand her. She considered herself too smart for the likes of Cornish.

The tide was coming in fast, and the cove would be underwater in no time. It was time to depart. The rocks below their feet were already far too wet and slippery. Paul Hicks body would wash up eventually. Cornish and Hutchens helped Emma negotiate the path back up to civilisation. As they reached the coastal footway, the sea engulfed the small cove.

Emma Hicks was assisted back to the national trust carpark. An ambulance had been called to collect the wounded and dead, but only one survivor was alive to tell the tale. Paul Hicks had succumbed to the perils of Carrick Roads. Another fatality to add to the statistics.

Darkness had descended on Carrick Roads, and the sheer madness of Paul Hicks demise had rattled everyone's cage. There would be no justice for the grieving families. Paul Hicks had chosen to take his own life rather than be incarcerated for eternity.

Cornish swore violently as she drove back from Carrick Roads. Hutchens remained silent rather than disturb the tirade. She knew better than to interrupt her boss.

Emma Hicks had been taken to Royal Cornwall Hospital in Truro to have her gunshot wound treated. She would remain overnight in the Duchy Hospital having insisted on a private room to recover from her ordeal. As she lay in bed, she smiled at the priceless way her brother had left this world. Paul thought he was a killer, he had tried to emulate her. He hadn't come close. There had been disappearances in the area over the years, and the police had been unable to find evidence to link any of the murders or missing persons to anybody. And they never would; she'd had a good mentor. Most people would think her as evil, a demon. She was capable of anything; a great manipulator and her grandfather had started this course of action. She had felt dirty, violated, hurt and ashamed that her grandfather had hurt her the way he did. She had wanted him to suffer. It had made her into an antisocial teenager placed on medication who had formed an identity which enabled her to cope with her past. She discovered that she enjoyed hurting others and killing them was power, putting her in control of their lives. She would kill again given the opportunity. It was in her blood. The recent killings had been a necessity, a means to an end, and Paul had been most complicit in his part. Mother would be proud.

Cornish walked into her cottage in the early hours. Englebert welcomed her as if she had been away forever.

She was exhausted. This case had taken over her life, and she felt cheated. Paul Hicks had escaped justice. She couldn't get her brain to shut up long enough to fall asleep. Mentally reviewing the day and previewing the day ahead left her mind reaching into the archives of past cases and events. Nothing was clear-cut about this case. Paul Hicks was a killer, but Cornish couldn't dismiss the nagging thought in her head. She was missing something. And she hadn't come this far to give up. Thinking about sleep and wishing for it to happen was a recipe for staying awake. This was where paradoxical thinking came in. Cornish got up and walked into her lounge where she kept her notebook. Writing down her thoughts helped her focus. Maggie and Nadine had suffered at the hands of their father. Emma and Paul had suffered at the hands of their grandfather. What other secrets were there? How many killers were there in just one family? Was there another killer lurking somewhere hidden in the shadows, a female perhaps? It was much easier to vilify a satanic, sinister femme fatale who acts callously and without remorse taking a life than it was to try and rain justice down on someone who was mentally ill and had been a victim of child sexual abuse. Cornish believed in good and evil; it was just not that simple. But it was an answer.

Chapter Fifty

Emma Hicks sat opposite Cornish and Pearce. Cornish wanted to clarify the events of the night Paul Hicks died. Cornish recited the police caution.

'You understand your rights?'

'Yes, I understand' replied Emma as a matter of fact. Clemo Nicholls adjusted the knot on his tie. A mannerism Cornish noticed when he was under pressure.

'Would you like to take us through the events leading up to your brother, Paul Hicks death?'

Emma recited her version of what happened. She and Paul had gone to the cottage to escape the constant media attention their family were receiving. She hadn't delivered the visual podcast to the media and had no knowledge of its existence. Paul had assumed rightly or wrongly that she had somehow betrayed him. Emma denied any knowledge of Paul as a cold and callous killer. Emma Hicks had nothing further to add or contribute other than she had loved her brother and they had both suffered in their childhood.

Cornish allowed Emma to take a short break before commencing their next session. She intended for this to be the last and she was looking forward to the grand finale.

Cornish looked at Emma Hicks as Pearce rolled in with the podcast. Cornish wanted to see Emma's reaction to the film. The production commenced. Emma sat in stony silence as Paul Hicks slaughtered Finley Jago for all to see. At the end Cornish regarded Emma.

'I must admit I missed it the first time I watched the podcast.'

Emma looked bewildered.

'Didn't you see it?'

Cornish was toying with her.

'I'm not sure what you mean.'

'The ring. The one you are wearing today and appear to never take off.'

Emma looked down at the diamond and sapphire ring. It had been her great-grandmother's, and she had worn it continuously since the day it had been bequeathed to her. Emma looked back with empty eyes. There was nothing. All evil murderers were missing something inside their heart, or maybe their soul, or both. The result was their eyes were blank.

'Didn't it ever occur to you that I like who I am, who I've become. I have never felt freer, liberated from the usual expectations and constraints of normal behaviour. I am a killer waiting to flourish and take my rightful place in society. I am at my finest when I kill testing my skills against you, the police and the authorities. The self that I want to be, desire, the voice inside my head. I am like two sides of the same coin, and both sides have now converged, and there is no going back.

I am my own law. Watching the light extinguish from my victims gives me incredible power. The look in their eyes is exquisite when they realise, they are going to die.'

It was as if a tap had been turned on. Emma Hicks clearly craved attention, or maybe she just didn't know what else to talk about other than her horrific pastime. She described her sickening crimes embellishing the details like an excited child.

'The intangible sensation that comes with watching someone take their last breath and knowing it's because of something I've done and enjoyed. Most people will never know how it feels to take another human life.'

Emma Hicks, head held high, was escorted from the interview room back to the cells. She wouldn't be granted bail. She was a clearly disturbed young woman.

'Take her away.'

Chapter Fifty-One

Emma Hicks made front page news. Cornwall was in the spotlight, and Cornish gave the best interview to date of her career. They celebrated in the pub after Jane Falconbridge congratulated them. They had done an excellent job, but it was still too late for those that had lost their lives.

Public opinion was divided on the reasons behind the murders once the family history of abuse was revealed. Emma and Paul Hicks past had made them the people they were, and others had consequently suffered and died. The consequences had lasted a lifetime and spanned generations. Events that had happened years ago had ensured that any future would be doomed to fail before it had even begun.

Cornish and her team had closed the case. There were no winners, only survivors, the families to carry the loss and burden of their loved ones into the future.

Clemo Nicholls job was made easier. Nadine Hicks and Barry Boscawen reached an understanding. They were equal partners in the running of the family estate. They were still family, after all.

Nadine Pascoe had lost both of her children. Paul's body washed up a week later not far from where he died. His body had been battered in Storm Hector, and Gilbert once more had the pleasure of accessing the course of death which was determined as death by misadventure. Paul Hicks funeral took place at Penmount Crematorium; the quiet ceremony held in the Trelawny Chapel. Nadine Pascoe and Barry Boscawen were the only family members present.

Cornish sat, once more, at the rear of the chapel. The police presence a mere formality. The chapel was empty except for the immediate family and their solicitor.

Clemo Nicholls sat solemnly wishing he wasn't the family solicitor. He would, given a choice, recant his remark that any publicity was better than no publicity. His reputation was in the toilet.

There was no real ceremony, no music, flowers or kind words publicly spoken.

Barry Boscawen watched Paul Hicks interned in his coffin enter his final destination. He felt nothing and had never liked his cousin. As the remaining family member from his mother's side, Barry felt obligated to attend. And he wanted the satisfaction of watching Paul Hicks enter the flames of hell.

Nadine Pascoe watched her only son's coffin rest within the catafalque. At the moment of committal, the curtains were slowly drawn, and Paul's body was removed from the earth. Nadine Pascoe showed no emotion whatsoever. She was now the High Priestess and leader of the Satanic group; her rightful position restored. The podcast had delivered the desired results. Her only thought was that in a few hours Paul Hicks ashes would be placed in a biodegradable urn and dispatched at sea, in the dark of the night. Somethings were better staying buried in the past where they belonged.

Chapter Fifty-Two

Cornish and her team had been tasked with the gruelling murders over the past few months. The police force had arrested the killers, and Emma Hicks now provided the main attraction in court. She relished her new-found fame as Cornwall's Carrick Roads killer. Cornish got her wish; Judge Barbara Smith would deliberate on the fate of Emma Hicks.

Hicks request for a trial by jury rather than a judge only trial was granted. Judge Barbara Smith would not be swayed by what had been reported in the media. This well-spoken public schoolgirl and educated posh bitch might look good on the stand, but Cornish knew she wouldn't be able to convince this Judge that she was innocent.

Clemo Nicholl declined the pleasure of defending his client citing personal health reasons. This was one case he wouldn't win. His reputation had been tarnished. Cornish watched the trial behind closed doors, and as Emma Hicks was taken away to serve her sentence, Cornwall could breathe a sigh of relief that this murderer would remain behind bars for life.

The team were exhausted. DCS Falconbridge congratulated them on their notable excellent results for Devon and Cornwall Police Force.

Jane Falconbridge updated Cornish following the Devon and Cornwall Police and Crime Panel meeting regarding the proposed merger with Dorset. The final decision had been made, and there would be no merger of Cornwall, Devon and Dorset. There were too many key concerns over the proposal and Cornish breathed a sigh of relief. Her team were far too stretched to incorporate more responsibility and work. Falconbridge couldn't agree more considering the challenging months the force had recently undertaken. This year had been the busiest on record so far. The police had already been overstretched with their hunt for the Pascoe family murderer and the Satanic cult killer and had arrested Steve Boscawen for the murder of his wife Maggie, Emma Hicks for her part in the killings of

Sonny, Derwa Moon and Finley Jago and Peter Chegwin for being an accomplish to the cult murders. The exceptionally hot weather combined with the influx of tourists and the excitement of the World Cup had provided additional challenges for the police.

Claire woke up the following day with a demonic hangover as a result of the lock-in in their regular public house and the celebration of the well-deserved results for the police. Saturday would be a whitewash consequently. Her head throbbed, and no number of tablets were going to have an immediate effect. Her eyes tried to adjust to the morning light as she attempted some relief by pressing on her third eye. She looked in the mirror. An older wilder version stared back, this last case had taken its toll. Claire groaned. Why had she had that extra glass of wine? Englebert was still sleeping. He could sleep all night without needing the toilet and most of the day. Claire was like a bear with a sore head. She needed some protein, something to help adhere to her stomach lining before attempting a long walk with Englebert along the coast path to their favourite place.

An hour later after a bacon butty and a cold shower, Claire felt ready to tackle the outside world. The opaque beauty Mother Nature created was incredible at this time of year. There was a real sense of autumn in the air, the crunching leaves had turned the colour of copper and lay scattered on the ground, and there was a smell of salty dampness from living by the coast. Claire donned her jacket and hat.

The sight sounds and the smell of autumn stirred Claire's soul. She felt sad which was not entirely unwelcome, a sort of sober, slowing down of her spirit, giving her time for reflection. Perhaps this was the time for Claire to consider new beginnings and try to reconnect and find her daughter. She had missed all the family gatherings over the years without her. Claire hadn't got a clue where she was. And the emptiness, she felt was unbearable. Claire felt nostalgic. This was the only season out of the four that she could honestly say made her the best version of herself, and maybe that was because it brought out the child in her. She felt this intense, emotionally charged, almost spiritual connection to autumn. Up until recently, she'd associated this feeling with the fact that she was born in October, and so was her daughter. She was reminded of her past. It should have been some of the best times of her life. Except it was filled with sad memories of her missing daughter. Not all was doom and gloom. Her career had transcended heights she never thought possible. That still hadn't filled the void of a husband and her daughter. With the leaves turning into other shades from deep green to burnt yellow and crimson something had shifted inside Claire. She became an entirely different person. And exactly the person she was meant to be and would like to be throughout the entire year. Autumn with its season of change and the next stage would this time prepare Claire to bring her closer to finding her daughter. She would put in motion definite plans.

As Claire and Englebert walked back to their cottage the whiff of smoke coming from a neighbour's chimney mingled with the dry leaves cluttering the ground. Piles of leaves hung around, and the trees looked like rainbows with their changing colours. The shifting sky moved from being sun-washed to storm-coloured as Claire and Englebert stepped through their front door. Instinctively Claire lit the fire and made herself a hot chocolate. The days were getting shorter as she snuggled up inside as the sea mist wrapped itself around the cottage like a blanket. This was Claire's refuge, a place where the biting cold couldn't follow, a safe place to retreat and be warm, safe and comfortable, her home.

Claire's headache had subsided, the fresh air had done its job. Claire reached for her notes. Work was never very far from her mind, and she had a backlog of paperwork to complete. She didn't hear the front door. Englebert looked up first, and Claire wondered who could be knocking on her day off.

Claire opened the door.
'Claire? Claire Cornish?'

'Yes, can I help you.'

'It's me, Jamie. Jamie Nance. Can I come in?'

Claire opened the door to allow Jamie to enter. The last time she had seen Jamie was the day after they had handed over their daughter for adoption. Claire had stayed in hospital breastfeeding her daughter for a week until the social worker took their child. Jamie had visited every day.

When she first met Jamie, it wasn't love at first sight, but it was definitely love within the first couple of hours. Claire had never met anyone since she had felt the same bond with. There were just so many subjects that they got onto somehow and saw them the same way every time. Sitting down together now years later it still held true. He was the same, Jamie.

Giving up their daughter hadn't ruined their lives, but it had been a wake-up call that had moved them both from childhood to adulthood. Adoption was the answer to the problem at the time and the solution that Claire and Jamie's parents only ever considered. Nobody died, the child lived. And the ongoing grief and feelings were still plainly evident. Neither had moved on. Jamie had a good career as a solicitor, but he'd never married and settled down. He had wanted to knock on Claire's door many times but had always backed out at the last moment. He'd watched Claire's career and read and listened to all her interviews in the media believing they would never be together again.

Claire and Jamie talked. The years slipped away as they laughed and cried. You couldn't control your attempt at reconciliation, yet Jamie's act of reaching out was reparative. They had shared some incredible moments together that were part of their identity, of who they were and forever in their hearts. They both wanted to find their daughter.

Jamie stayed until the early hours. He was stopping in a local Airbnb and promised to return the next day.

Claire felt like an excited teenager again. Exhausted, relieved, she realised Jamie was the one that got away. She wished she could turn back time and change all that had happened. She couldn't. They had to move forward. They weren't the same people, but that was OK. They still cared and had feelings for each other. That much was obvious. Only time would tell, and they had plenty of that.

They spent Sunday together reminiscing about the past and discussing the future. Jamie wanted to move back to Cornwall. He had been offered a partnership in Truro. Before he took the position, he had wanted to see Claire and discuss if there was any possibility of rekindling their friendship and possibly finding their daughter. He wasn't expecting anything more from Claire, but he was hoping it might lead to something more serious.

Claire was sad to see Jamie leave at the end of the weekend. They had made firm plans and Claire knew deep down that Jamie would be her rock.

When Claire walked into work on Monday morning, Hutchens looked up and smiled.

'It looks like someone had a good weekend?'

'The best.' Was all Claire could say before the call came in.

A body has been found at Highcliff.

Copyright © FG Laycy 2019

The right of FG Laycy to be identified as the author of this work has been asserted in accordance with the Copyright, Designs and Patents Act 1988.

All rights reserved. No part of this publication may be reproduced, stored in or transmitted into any retrieval system, in any form, or by any means (electronic, mechanical, photocopying, or recording or otherwise) without the prior written permission of the publisher.

Any person who does any unauthorised act in relation to this publication may be liable to criminal prosecution and civil claims for damages.

This is a work of fiction. Any resemblance to actual persons living and dead is purely coincidental.

ISBN Printed Book: 9781090299475

Imprint: Independently Published

Cover design copyright © FG Laycy

Author's Note

Although this book is very much a work of fiction, Carrick Roads is a real area and is located in spectacular Cornwall. The county has provided inspiration for many novels and television series over the years and is steeped in history.

The names of places have been preserved to bring realistic licence to the plot and to truly describe the wonderful and really beautiful qualities that Cornwall has to offer. My characters are fictitious and any resemblance to real persons, living or dead, is purely coincidental.

The cover image portrays Carrick Roads and St Anthony's lighthouse, the setting for the climactic scene of the story.

Bio

Born in Kenilworth, Warwickshire, FG Laycy moved to Worcester and Coventry to train and become a State Registered Nurse. After working in nursing for a few years, she moved to Russia with her family and remained there for eleven years before relocating to Cornwall.

She now divides her time between Cornwall and France.

FG Laycy is the author of the Hunter Mackenzie series, her debut thriller novel, *The Tenth Congress*, was released in October 2017 on Amazon Kindle UK and her second novel *The Day of Reckoning* was released in August 2018.

The novels are available to purchase in e-book and paperback on the Amazon store.

Acknowledgements

As with all the best things in life, they are never to be enjoyed alone. Special thanks to those friends and family for their input along the way. Lastly but by no means least, to my lovely husband Martin, for his continued support especially in the kitchen.

Other fiction books by F G Laycy

The Tenth Congress

The Day of Reckoning

Non-fiction books by Fiona G Laycy

Women on Top, 69 Positions to Success

Printed in Great Britain
by Amazon